ESSENTI

Shipment One

A Little Bit Country
Country Bride
Wanted: Perfect Partner
Cindy and the Prince
Some Kind of Wonderful
The Courtship of Carol Sommars

Shipment Two

Navy Wife
Navy Blues
Navy Brat
Navy Woman
Navy Baby
Navy Husband

Shipment Three

Yours and Mine
The Bachelor Prince
Denim and Diamonds
The Wyoming Kid
The Man You'll Marry
Marriage Wanted
Laughter in the Rain

Shipment Four

The Cowboy's Lady
The Sheriff Takes a Wife
Marriage of Inconvenience
Stand-In Wife
Bride on the Loose
Same Time, Next Year

Shipment Five

Rainy Day Kisses
Mail-Order Bride
The Matchmakers
Father's Day
A Friend or Two
No Competition

Shipment Six

First Comes Marriage
White Lace and Promises
Friends—and Then Some
The Way to a Man's Heart
Hasty Wedding
That Wintry Feeling
Those Christmas Angels

Shipment Seven

Borrowed Dreams
Starlight
Promise Me Forever
Shadow Chasing
For All My Tomorrows
The Playboy and the Widow

Shipment Eight

Fallen Angel
Yesterday's Hero
Reflections of Yesterday
All Things Considered
The Trouble With Caasi
Almost Paradise

The
ESSENTIAL COLLECTION

#1 *New York Times* Bestselling Author

DEBBIE MACOMBER

Mail-Order BRIDE

◊ HARLEQUIN®
™ESSENTIAL DEBBIE MACOMBER COLLECTION

Recycling programs
for this product may
not exist in your area.

ISBN-13: 978-0-373-47298-7

MAIL-ORDER BRIDE

Copyright © 1987 by Debbie Macomber

Printed in U.S.A.

DEBBIE MACOMBER

is a number one *New York Times* and *USA TODAY* best-selling author. Her books include *1225 Christmas Tree Lane, 1105 Yakima Street, A Turn in the Road, Hannah's List* and *Debbie Macomber's Christmas Cookbook,* as well as *Twenty Wishes, Summer on Blossom Street* and *Call Me Mrs. Miracle.* She has become a leading voice in women's fiction worldwide and her work has appeared on every major bestseller list, including those of the *New York Times, USA TODAY, Publishers Weekly* and *Entertainment Weekly.* She is a multiple award winner, and won the 2005 Quill Award for Best Romance. There are more than one hundred million copies of her books in print. Two of her Harlequin MIRA Christmas titles have been made into Hallmark Channel Original Movies, and the Hallmark Channel has launched a series based on her bestselling Cedar Cove series. For more information on Debbie and her books, visit her website, www.debbiemacomber.com.

In memory of Ron Cowden
and for his son, Max,
beloved New Zealand friends

Prologue

"I'm so worried about dear Caroline," Ethel Myers murmured thoughtfully, sipping tea from a dainty porcelain cup. Her fingers clutched a delicate lace-trimmed handkerchief and when a droplet of moisture formed in the corner of her eye, she dabbed it gently. "Sister, I do believe the brew is stronger today."

"Yes," Mabel admitted. "But remember what Father said about the brew enhancing one's ability to solve problems."

"And we must do something to help Caroline."

Mabel shook her head sadly. "Perhaps if you and I had married suitable gentlemen all those years ago…"

"Oh, yes, then maybe we'd know how to help that sweet, sweet child." Ethel's faded blue eyes brightened momentarily. "You do remember that George Guettermann once asked for my hand."

"As I recall, Mother was quite impressed with him."

Ethel's shoulders sagged. "But Father was suspicious from the first."

Mabel sighed heavily. "Mr. Guettermann did cut such a dashing figure."

A wistful expression marked Ethel's fragile features. "If only he hadn't already been married."

"The scoundrel!"

"We must learn to forgive him, Sister."

Mabel nodded and lifted the steaming pot of brew. "I was thinking of Caroline's young man. Another cup, Sister?"

"Oh dear, should we?" Ethel's hand flew to her mouth to smother a loud hiccup, and she had the good grace to look embarrassed.

"We *must* find a way to help her."

"Yes," Ethel agreed as Mabel filled her cup to the bright gold rim. "Poor, poor Caroline."

"There was something in his eyes."

"George?"

"No, Sister. Caroline's young man."

"Indeed, there was something about his eyes." Ethel took another sip and lightly patted her chest at the strength of their father's special recipe. "Sister, the brew…"

"We must think!"

"Oh, yes. Think. What can we do for dear Caroline?"

"If only her mother were alive."

"Or grandmother."

"Grandmother?"

"Her great-great-grandmother, perhaps. *She* would know what to do." Ethel smiled. "Do you recall how she frowned on courting? Said it simply wasn't necessary."

"Grandmother would. Asa Myers brought her to Seattle with the other mail-order brides. She and Grandfather knew each other less than twenty-four hours before they were married."

"A courtship wasn't necessary and they were so happy."

"Very happy and very compatible."

"With seven children, they must have agreed quite nicely," Ethel said and giggled delightedly.

"It's such a shame marriages aren't arranged these days," Mabel said, taking another long sip of tea.

"If only we could find Caroline a husband."

"But, Sister…" Mabel was doubtful. For over fifty years they'd been unable to find husbands of their own. So how could they expect to come up with one for their beloved niece?

Ethel's hand shook as she lowered the cup to its saucer. "Sister, Sister! I do believe I have the solution." Her voice quavered with excitement as she reached for the morning paper.

"Yes?"

"Our own Caroline will be a mail-order bride."

Mabel frowned. "But things like that aren't done in this day and age."

Ethel fumbled with the paper until she located the classified section. She folded back the unwieldy page and pointed to the personal column. "Here, read this."

Mabel read the ad aloud, her voice trembling. "Wanted—Wife for thirty two-year-old Alaskan male. Send picture. Transportation provided." The advertisement included the name Paul Trevor and a box number.

"But Sister, do we dare?"

"We must. Caroline is desperately unhappy."

"And she did have the opportunity to select a husband of her own."

"She chose poorly. The beast left her standing at the altar."

"The scoundrel!"

"We mustn't tell her, of course."

"Oh, no, we can't let her know. Our Caroline would object strenuously."

"Sister, I do believe the brew has helped."

"Indeed! Some more?"

Ethel raised her cup and her older sister automatically refilled it. A smile of satisfaction lifted the edges of her mouth. "Father's recipe was most beneficial."

"It always is, Sister."

"Oh, yes. Yes, indeed."

One

Caroline Myers waited at a Starbucks in the Seattle-Tacoma airport, accompanied by her great-aunts. She could hardly believe she would soon depart the state of Washington for unknown adventures in Alaska.

"Do you have everything, dear?" Mabel asked her for the third time.

"Aunt Ethel, Aunt Mabel, please —I can't allow you to do this."

"Nonsense," Ethel said briskly. "This vacation is our gift to you."

"But Alaska in October?"

"It's lovely, dear heart. I promise."

"Yes, lovely," Ethel agreed, trying to hide a smile. "And we have the nicest surprise waiting for you."

Caroline stared suspiciously at her great-aunts. Something that could only be mischief danced in their sparkling blue eyes. At seventy-nine and eighty, they were her only living relatives in Seattle, and she loved them dearly. Despite their age, she'd always called them simply *aunt*.

"But this trip is too much," she said.

"Nonsense."

"Hurry, dear. Go and check in or you'll miss your plane."

"One question."

Ethel and Mabel exchanged fleeting glances. "Yes?"

"Why the blood tests? I didn't know anything like that was necessary for travel within the United States."

Mabel paused to clear her throat,

casting her eyes wildly about the terminal. "It's a new law."

"A gubernatorial decision, I…I believe," Ethel stammered.

"It's such a pity," Mabel said, changing the subject. "We wanted to give you a thermos with Father's special tea to sustain you during the flight, but all these rules…" She shook her head.

"It's probably just as well," Caroline said, doing her utmost to swallow a chuckle. She'd been eighteen when she'd first discovered the potency of her great-grandfather's special recipe.

"We put some sandwiches in that bag, though." Ethel pointed at the duffel the aunts had packed for her. "Plus tea for when you land. And a little something extra."

Caroline smiled her thanks, feeling a bit foolish about dragging food, not to mention the "tea," all the way to Alaska. She wondered if the duffel with its special wares would survive the baggage handlers.

"Do write. And call," Mabel said anxiously.

"Of course. I'll send postcards." Caroline kissed both aunts on the cheek and hugged them gently. Ethel sniffled, and Mabel cast her a look of sisterly displeasure. Caroline grinned. Her two great-aunts had been a constant delight all her life. They were charming, loving and thoroughly enchanting. They'd done everything they could to cheer her after Larry's defection. The sudden memory of the man she'd loved with such intensity produced a fresh wave of pain that threatened to wash away the pleasure of this moment.

Ethel sniffled again. "We shall miss you dreadfully," she announced, glaring at her sister.

Caroline threw back her head and laughed aloud. "I'm only going to be gone a week." Ethel's and Mabel's eyes avoided hers and Caroline wondered what little game they were playing.

"But a week seems so long."

"You have your ticket?" Mabel asked hurriedly.

"Right here." Caroline patted the side of her purse.

"Remember, a nice young man will be meeting you in Fairbanks."

Caroline nodded. Her aunts had gone over the details of this vacation a minimum of fifty times. "And he's taking me to—"

"Gold River," the great-aunts chimed in, bobbing their heads in unison.

"There I'll be met by—"

"Paul Trevor." Ethel and Mabel shared a silly grin.

"Right, Paul Trevor." Caroline studied her aunts surreptitiously. If she didn't know better, she'd think they had something up their sleeves. For days, the two of them had been acting like giddy teen-agers, whispering and giggling. Caroline had objected to this vacation from the first; Alaska in early October wasn't exactly her first choice. She wouldn't have argued nearly as much had they suggested Hawaii, but her aunts had been so insistent on Alaska that Caroline had finally agreed. This was their gift to her in an effort to heal a broken heart, and she wasn't about to ruin it by being stubborn. She couldn't bear to inform them that it would take a whole lot more than a trip north for her heart to mend.

Caroline hugged her aunts and se-cured her purse strap over her shoul-der, then got up to join the line at the airline counter.

"Do be happy, dear," Ethel said tear-fully, pressing her frilly lace handker-chief under her nose.

Mabel's voice seemed strained as she

echoed her sister's words and clasped Caroline's free hand. "Happiness, child. Much, much happiness."

Shaking her head at their strange behavior, Caroline checked in, went through Security and dropped off her bags. She got to the departure lounge without much time to spare. Ten minutes later, she entered the long, narrow jetway that led to the Boeing 767. The flight attendant directed her to the business section and, again, Caroline had to wonder how her aunts could possibly afford this trip.

Ethel and Mabel left the airport pleased with themselves yet already missing their beloved niece.

"It's fate, Sister," Mabel said softly.

"Oh, indeed. Paul Trevor chose her over all those other women."

"He sounds like such a good man."

"And so handsome."

"Only he wrote that he has a beard now. Does Caroline like men with beards?"

Ethel shrugged. "I really couldn't say."

"She'll grow to love him."

"Oh, yes. Given time, she'll be very happy with Paul."

"Perhaps she'll be as compatible with him as Grandmother was with Grandfather."

"Seven children. Oh, Sister!" Ethel brought her gloved hands to her rosy cheeks.

Doubts vanished and the two exchanged a brilliant smile.

"We did our best for her," Mabel said happily. "Her mother would've been proud."

"Her great-great-grandmother, too," Ethel said, and as they giggled with pure delight, several onlookers cast curious glances in their direction.

* * *

Caroline slept for most of the night flight to Fairbanks. She was exhausted from a hectic week at work. As a nurse for Dr. Kenneth James, an internist, she often put in long days. Dr. James gave her the week off without complaint and then, on Friday afternoon, shook her hand and wished her much happiness. Now that she thought about it, Caroline found his words puzzling. Vacations were about fun. Happiness came from having a satisfactory relationship. Like hers and Larry's... His name drifted into her mind with such ease that Caroline shook her head in an effort to dismiss it.

Straightening in her seat, she opened her eyes. The cabin lights were dimmed, and the only other passenger in business class was asleep. The two attendants were drinking coffee, but when one of them noticed that Caroline was awake, she immediately approached her.

"You missed the meal. Would you care for something to eat now?"

Caroline shook her head. "No, thanks."

The tall brunette responded with a smile and a slight nod and returned to her coffee. Caroline watched as she walked away. Maybe this flight attendant was the type of woman her ex-fiancé should marry, she mused. She'd known from the beginning how completely dissimilar Larry's and her tastes were. Larry liked late, late nights and breakfast in bed, while she was a morning person, eager to begin each new day. Caroline enjoyed the outdoor life— hiking, camping, boating. Larry's idea of roughing it was doing without valet service. She liked cornflakes with chocolate syrup poured over the top and spaghetti for breakfast. Larry preferred formal dinners with nothing more exotic than meat and potatoes. And those were just the superficial differences between them. But they'd loved each other enough to believe they could compromise. *She* had loved *him*, Caroline corrected herself. At the last minute, Larry had buckled under his doubts and had sent his witless brother to contact her an hour before the wedding ceremony. Once again, humiliation engulfed her.

For the first week, Caroline had hidden from the world. Her two beloved aunts had hovered over her constantly, insisting that she eat and sleep, taking her temperature in case she developed what they called the ague. Caroline assumed it must be some kind of fever and allowed them to fret over her. At the time, it would've taken more energy to assure them she was fine than to submit to their tender ministrations.

A month passed and Caroline gradually worked her way out of the heavy depression that had hung over her like a thundercloud. She smiled and laughed, but suspected that her aunts were unconvinced. Every time she was with them, they stuck a thermometer under her tongue and shook their gray heads with worried frowns.

Larry called her only once to stammer his regrets and to apologize repeatedly. If she hadn't been so much in love with him, she might've been able to accept that he'd probably done them both a favor. Now there were whole hours when she didn't think about him, or hunger for information about him, or long to be held in his arms. Still, the thought of him with another woman was almost more than Caroline could tolerate. In time, however, she would learn to accept that as well.

The disaster with Larry had taught her that she possessed a far stronger constitution than she'd ever believed. She'd been able to hold her head high and return to work a week after the aborted wedding. It hadn't been easy, but she'd done it with a calm maturity that impressed even her. She was going to come out of this a much wiser, more discerning woman. Someday there'd be a man who would love her enough to appreciate her sometimes unconventional ways. When they fell in love, she'd think about marriage again. But not for a long time, Caroline decided— not for a very long time.

As the plane descended into Fairbanks, Caroline gathered her jacket and her purse, preparing to disembark. It was still dark, but dawn was starting to streak the sky. Just as her aunts had promised, there was someone waiting for her at the airport. She had no sooner walked off the plane than a middle-aged man with bushy eyebrows and a walrus mustache held up a piece of cardboard with her name printed across it in bold letters.

"Hello, I'm Caroline Myers," she told him, shifting her purse from one hand to the other.

"Welcome to Alaska," he said with a wide grin and offered his hand. "Name's John Morrison."

Caroline shook it. She liked him immediately. "Thank you, John."

The man continued to stare at her and rubbed the side of his square jaw. Slowly, he shook his head and a sly grin raised the edges of his mouth. "Paul did all right for himself," he mumbled.

"Pardon?"

"Ah, nothing," John responded, shaking his head again. "I'm just surprised is all. I didn't expect him to come up with anyone half as attractive as you. I don't suppose you have a friend?"

Caroline hadn't the faintest idea

what this burly bush pilot was getting at, or why he'd be curious about her friends. Surely he'd flown more than one woman into the Alaskan interior. She was like any other tourist visiting Alaska for a one-week stay. She planned to get plenty of rest and relaxation on the direct orders of her aunts. In addition, she hoped to take invigorating walks and explore the magic of the tundra. Her aunts had mentioned Paul Trevor's name on several occasions and Caroline assumed they'd hired him as her guide. She wouldn't mind having someone show her the countryside. There was so much to see and do, and Caroline was ready for it all.

Once John had collected her suitcase, plus the duffel bag her aunts had so determinedly packed, he escorted Caroline to the single-engine Cessna and helped her climb aboard.

"Won't be long now," he said, placing

the earphones over his head and flipping several switches. As he zipped up his fur-lined coat, he glanced in her direction with a frown. Then the control tower issued instructions and John turned his attention to the radio. Once on the runway, the plane accelerated and was soon aiming for the dawn sky in a burst of power that had Caroline clenching her hands. She was accustomed to flying, but not in anything quite this small. In comparison to the wide-bodied jet, this Cessna seemed tiny and fragile.

"You might want to look in some of those boxes back there." He jerked his head toward the large pile of sacks and cardboard boxes resting next to her suitcase at the rear of the plane.

"Uh, what should I be looking for?"

"A coat. It's going to get damn cold up here. That little jacket's never gonna be warm enough."

"Okay." Caroline unfastened the seat belt and turned around to bend over the back of her seat. She sorted through the sacks and found a variety of long underwear and flannel shirts.

"Paul's right about you needing this. I hope the boots fit. I got the best available."

"Boots?"

"Lady, trust me. You're going to need them."

"I imagine they were expensive." She had her credit cards with her, but if Paul Trevor expected her to pick up the tab on a complete winter wardrobe, then he had another think coming.

Caroline pulled out a thick coat, but it was so bulky that she placed it over her knees. She took off her jacket and slipped her arms into a cozy flannel shirt. She'd put on the coat when they landed.

"What did you bring with you?" John

asked, eyeing the duffel bag at Caroline's feet.

She rolled her eyes. "My aunts sent along some food."

John chuckled.

Now that she'd mentioned it, Caroline discovered she was hungry. It'd been hours since she'd last eaten, and her stomach growled as she opened the bag to find half a dozen thick sandwiches and—the promised thermos. There was also a brightly wrapped gift. Somewhat surprised, Caroline removed the package and tore off the bright paper and ribbon. The sheer negligee with the neckline and sleeves trimmed in faux fur baffled her even more.

John saw her blink and laughed loudly. "I see they included something to keep your neck warm."

Caroline found his humor less than amusing and stuffed the gown back inside the bag. She'd never thought of her aunts as senile, but their recent behavior gave her cause to wonder.

She shared a turkey sandwich with John and listened as he spoke at length about Alaska. His love for this last frontier was apparent in every sentence. His comments included a vivid description of the tundra and its varied wildlife.

"I have a feeling you're going to like it here."

"Well, I like what little I've seen," Caroline said. She'd expected the land to be barren and harsh. It was, but there was a majestic beauty about it that made Caroline catch her breath.

"That's Denali over there," John told her. "She's the highest peak in North America."

"I thought McKinley was."

"Folks around here prefer to call her Denali."

"What's that?" Caroline pointed to

the thin silver ribbon that stretched across the rugged countryside below.

"The Yukon River. She flows over two thousand miles from northwest Canada to the Bering Sea."

"Wow."

"Anything you'd like to know about Paul?"

"Paul Trevor? Not really. Is there anything I *should* know?" Like her aunts, John seemed to bring up the other man's name at every opportunity.

He gave another merry chuckle. "Guess you'll be finding out about him soon enough."

"Right." She eyed him curiously. She was anxious to get a look at this man who insisted she have all this costly gear.

"He's a quiet guy. Hope you don't mind that."

"I usually chatter enough for two. I

think we'll get along fine. Besides, I don't plan on being here that long."

John frowned. "I doubt you'll ever get Paul to leave Alaska."

Caroline was offended by the brusque tone. "I don't have any intention of trying."

The amusement faded from John's rugged face as he checked the instruments on the front panel. "You aren't afraid of flying, are you?"

She hadn't thought about it much until now. "Afraid? Why should I be afraid?"

"Looks like we may be headed into a storm. Nothing to worry about, but this could be a real roller-coaster for a while."

"I'll be fine." The sudden chill in the cabin caused Caroline to reach for the thermos. "My aunts make a mean cup of tea. Interested?"

"No, thanks." He focused on the

gauges. Caroline refastened her seat belt, fingers trembling.

The first cup of spiked tea brought a rush of warmth to her chilled arms, and when the plane pitched and heaved, she carefully refilled the plastic cup and gulped down a second. "Hey, this is fun," she said with a tiny laugh twenty minutes later. If the truth be known, she was frightened out of her wits, but she put on a brave front and held on to her drink with both hands. Her aunts' tea was courage in a cup.

By the time John announced that they were within a half hour of Gold River, Caroline felt as warm as toast. As they made their descent, she peeked out the window at the uneven row of houses. A blanket of snow covered the ground and curling rings of smoke rose from a dozen chimneys.

"It's not much of a town, is it?" she murmured.

"Around three hundred. Mostly Athabascans—they're Indians who were once nomadic, following caribou and other game. When the white settlers arrived, they established permanent villages. Nowadays, they mostly hunt and fish. Once we get a bit closer you'll see a string of caribou hides drying in the sun."

"How…interesting." Caroline had no idea how else to respond.

"What does Paul do?" she asked a few minutes later.

John gave her a curious stare. "Don't you know? He works for the oil company. Keeps tabs on the pump station for the pipeline."

She brushed aside the blond curl that fell over her face. "I thought he was a guide of some sort."

As the Cessna circled the village, Caroline saw people scurrying out of the houses. Several raised their arms high above their heads and waved. "They see us," she said.

"They've probably spent days preparing for your arrival."

"How thoughtful." The village must only entertain a handful of tourists a year, she figured, and residents obviously went to a great deal of trouble to make sure that those who did come felt welcome. Caroline rubbed her eyes. The whole world seemed to be whirling. The people and houses blurred together and she shook her head, hoping to regain her bearings. The thermos was empty; Caroline realized she was more than a little intoxicated.

A glance at the darkening clouds produced a loud grumble from John. "Doesn't look like I'm going to be able to stick around for the reception."

"I'm sorry." John was probably a local hero. This welcoming party was likely as much in his honor as hers. It appeared that the entire village was outside now, with everyone pointing toward the sky and waving enthusiastically. "I don't see a runway."

"There isn't one."

"But..."

"There's enough of a clearing to make a decent landing. I've come down in a lot worse conditions."

Caroline's nails cut into her palm. She didn't find his words all that reassuring. Why her aunts would choose such a remote village for her vacation was beyond her. This whole trip was turning into much more of an adventure than she'd ever dreamed—or wanted.

As the plane descended, she closed her eyes until she felt the wheels bounce on the uneven ground. She was jostled, jolted and jarred, but otherwise unscathed. Once they came to a complete stop, Caroline could breathe again.

The single engine continued to purr

as John unhooked his seat belt. "Go ahead and climb out. I'll hand you the gear."

Using her shoulder to push open the airplane door, Caroline nearly fell to the snow, despite her effort to climb down gracefully. A gust of wind sobered her instantly. "It's cold!"

"Yeah, but Paul will warm you," John shouted over the engine's noise. He tossed out her suitcase and a large variety of boxes and sacks. "Good luck to you. I have a feeling you're the best thing to happen to Paul in a long time."

"Thanks." She stood in the middle of the supplies and blinked twice. "Aren't you coming with me?"

"Can't. I've got to get out of here before this storm hits." He shut the door and a minute later was taxiing away.

With a sense of disbelief, Caroline watched him leave. Already she could see several snowmobiles and a team of dogs pulling a large sled racing toward her. She waved on the off-chance they couldn't see her. Again the earth seemed to shift beneath her feet, and she rubbed her eyes in an effort to maintain her balance. Good grief, just how much of that tea had she drunk?

By the time the first dogsled arrived, she'd mustered a smile. "Hello," she greeted, raising her hand, praying no one would guess she was more than a little tipsy.

"Welcome."

The man, who must be Paul Trevor, walked toward her and handed her a small bouquet of flowers. He was tall and dark, and from what she could see of his bearded face, reasonably attractive. Untamed curls fell with rakish disregard across a wide, intelligent brow. His eyes, as blue as her own, gazed at her critically. She'd taken to John Morrison immediately, but Caroline wasn't sure she'd like this man. John had spoken of him with respect, and it was obvious that he was considered a leader among the villagers. But his intensity unnerved her. Caroline wasn't about to let him intimidate her; however, now wasn't the time to say much of anything. Not when her tongue refused to cooperate with her brain.

"Thank you." Caroline closed her eyes as she smelled the flowers, expecting the sweet scent of spring, only to have her nose tickled by the prickly needles. She gave a startled gasp and her eyes flew open.

"They've been dried."

"Oh." She felt like a fool. There weren't any flowers in Alaska this time of year. "Of course—they must be."

"Everything's ready if you are."

"Sure." Caroline assumed he was speaking of the welcoming reception. The large group of people quickly loaded her suitcase and the other boxes onto several sleds. Caroline took a step toward Paul and nearly stumbled. Again the ground pitched under her feet. She recognized it as the potency of the tea and not an earthquake, but for a moment she was confused. "I'm sorry," she murmured. "I seem to be a bit unsteady."

Paul guided her to the dogsled. "It might be better if you sat." He pulled back a heavy blanket and helped her into the sled. A huge husky, clearly the lead dog, turned his head to examine her and Caroline grinned sheepishly. "I don't weigh much," she told him and giggled. Then she groaned. She was beginning to sound like her aunts.

The trip into Gold River took only minutes. Paul helped her out of the sled and led her into the long narrow building in the center of the village. Candles flickered all around the room. Tables filled with a variety of dishes lined the walls. A priest, Russian Orthodox, Caroline guessed, wore a long gold robe. He smiled at her warmly and stepped forward to greet her, taking her hand in his.

"Welcome to Gold River. I'm Father Nabokov."

"I'm pleased to meet you, Father." Caroline prayed that he didn't smell her aunts' brew on her breath.

"Are you hungry?" Paul had shed his thick coat and she removed hers, passing it to him. The force of his personality was revealed in his stance. On meeting him, Caroline understood why both John and her two aunts had found occasion to mention Paul. His personality was strong, but there was a gentleness as well, a tenderness he preferred to disguise with the sense of remoteness she'd noticed earlier.

"Hungry? No...not really," she replied tentatively, realizing that she was staring at him. Paul didn't seem to mind. For that matter, he appeared to be sizing her up as well, and judging by the lazy, sensual smile that moved from his mouth to his eyes, he seemed to like what he saw.

If only Caroline could have cleared her mind, she felt she might've been able to strike up a witty conversation, but her thoughts were preoccupied with the murmuring around her. It looked as though the entire village was crammed inside the meeting hall. Someone was playing music, but it wasn't on an instrument Caroline recognized. A fiddle player joined the first man and the festive mood spread until everyone was laughing and singing. Several helped themselves to plates and heaped food on them from the serving dishes.

"Perhaps it would be best if we started things now," Father Nabokov suggested.

"It doesn't look like we'll be able to hold things up much longer."

"Do you mind?" Paul glanced at Caroline.

"Not in the least. Why wait?" Nearly everyone was eating and drinking as it was, and she could see no reason to delay the party. Someone brought her a glass of champagne and Caroline drank it down in one big swallow. The room was warm and she was so thirsty. The hardest part was keeping her eyes open; her lids felt exceptionally heavy and, without much effort, she could have crawled into bed and slept for a month.

Paul raised his hand and the music stopped, followed by instant silence. The townspeople shuffled forward, forming a large circle around Paul, Caroline and the priest.

Caroline smiled and closed her eyes, awaiting the announcement that was obviously forthcoming. She felt so relaxed. These wonderful, wonderful people were holding some kind of ceremony to welcome her. If only she could stay awake...

Father Nabokov began speaking in a soft, reverent voice. The smell of incense filled the air. She made an honest effort to listen, but the priest's words were low and monotonous. The others in the room seemed to give heed to his message, whatever it was, and Caroline glanced around, smiling now and then.

"Caroline?" Paul's voice cut into her musings.

"Hmm." She realized the meeting hall was quiet, each face regarding her expectantly as though waiting for a response. Paul slipped an arm around her waist, pulling her closer to his side.

"Would you like him to repeat the question?" Paul asked, studying her with a thoughtful frown.

"Yes, please," Caroline said quietly. If

she knew what these people expected of her, then maybe she could reply. "What did he say?"

"He's asking if you'll honor and cherish me."

Two

"Honor and cherish?" Caroline repeated, stunned. This reception was more than she could grasp. How she wished she hadn't had quite so much of her aunts' brew. Obviously this little get-together in her honor was some kind of elaborate charade—one in which Caroline had no intention of participating.

The circle of faces stared anxiously, growing more and more distressed at the length of time it took her to respond to the question.

"Caroline?" Even Paul's gruff voice revealed his uneasiness.

Caroline opened her mouth to tell them that if they were going to play silly tricks on her, she didn't want anything to do with this party. She looked at Paul and blinked. "I thought you were supposed to be my guide." Apparently folks took the guiding business seriously in these parts.

Father Nabokov smiled gently. "He will guide you throughout your life, my child."

A clatter rose from the crowd as several people started arguing loudly. Father Nabokov raised his arms above his head and waved. "Miss Myers." He paused to wipe his brow with a clean kerchief that magically appeared from inside his huge sleeve. "This is an important decision. Would you like me to ask the question again?"

Paul's intense blue eyes cleared as his

gaze pinned hers, demanding that she answer the priest.

An older man, an Athabascan who was apparently a good friend of Paul's, interceded. "You can't back down now—you already agreed."

"I did?" What had her aunts gotten her into? The other guests continued to glare at her and Caroline felt unsettled by the resentment she saw in their eyes. "Could I have something cold to drink?"

"It's a bit unusual," Father Nabokov said, frowning. For the second time, he reached for the kerchief and rubbed it over his forehead.

"Walter," Paul called to the older man, who immediately stepped forward.

A minute later, he approached them with a glass of champagne, which Paul handed to Caroline. She hurriedly emptied it and sighed audibly as the bubbles tickled the back of her throat. She returned her glass to the man Paul had called Walter and smiled. "This is excellent champagne."

Walter nodded abruptly and glanced in Paul's direction. "Paul wanted the best for you."

Feeling uneasy, Caroline noted the censure in the old man's voice. "What was it you wanted me to say again?"

Paul's posture stiffened as he expelled an impatient sigh. "*Yes* would suffice."

"All right then," she agreed in an attempt to be as amicable as possible. Everyone had gone to so much trouble on her behalf, cooking and planning this reception for her arrival. She hated to disappoint them, although she wondered if all tourists were graced with this kind of party—the priest, the champagne, not to mention the presence of the entire village. Her adorable aunts had sent her to the one place in the world where she'd be welcomed with an ardor befitting royalty.

"You do?" Father Nabokov looked greatly relieved.

"Sure," she concurred brightly, shrugging her shoulders. "Why not?"

"Indeed." The priest grinned, then turned to Paul. His eyes glowed as he gazed upon them both. Caroline felt Paul slide his arm around her once again, but she didn't object. She attempted to give the priest her full attention, but the room was so warm.... She fanned her face and with some difficulty kept a stiff smile on her lips.

Paul took her hand and slipped a simple gold band on her ring finger. It looked like a friendship ring and Caroline thought it a lovely gesture.

"I now pronounce you husband and wife," Father Nabokov proclaimed solemnly. He raised his right hand, blessing them both. "You may kiss the bride."

Wife! Kiss the bride! Caroline was completely shocked. She tried to smile, but couldn't. "What's he talking about?" she muttered.

Paul didn't answer. Instead, he turned her in his arms and his eyes narrowed longingly on her mouth. Before she could voice her questions and uncertainties, he lowered his head. Caroline's heart thundered nervously and she placed her hands on his chest, gazing up at his bearded face. Surely he could tell how confused she was. A wedding ceremony! She must be dreaming. That was it—this was all a dream. Paul's blue eyes softened. Gradually, as though in slow motion, his mouth settled warmly over hers. His touch was firm and experienced, moist and gentle—ever so gentle. *Nice dream,* Caroline mused, *very nice, very real.* She hadn't expected a man of his size to be so tender.

Enjoy it, girl, she thought, kissing him back. Dreams ended far too quickly. The world began to spin, so she slipped her arms around Paul's neck to help maintain her balance. Bringing her body closer to his was all the encouragement he needed. His hands slid over her hips, pressing her body invitingly against his own. Caroline surrendered willingly to the sensual upheaval. Ever since Larry had left her at the altar, she'd been dying to be held in a man's arms, dying to be kissed as if there was no moment but this one.

Father Nabokov cleared his throat, but Caroline paid no heed to the priest's disapproval. She might have had her doubts about Paul, but she had to admit he was one great kisser. Breathless, they broke apart, still staring at each other, lost in the wonder of their overwhelming response.

Paul draped his wrists over Caroline's shoulders. A slightly cynical smile touched his mouth. "For a minute there, I didn't think you were going through with it."

"Is this a dream?" Caroline asked.

Paul gave her a funny look. "No."

She laughed. "Of course you'd say that."

His eyes were as blue as anything Caroline had ever seen and she felt as though she was drowning in their depths. She managed a tremulous smile, her mouth still on fire from his kiss. Involuntarily, she moistened her lips and watched as his eyes darkened.

"Let's get out of here," he growled. Without another word, he hauled Caroline into his arms and stalked toward the door.

Caroline gasped at the unexpectedness of the action, but the villagers went crazy, resuming their dancing and singing. "Where…where are we going?"

"The cabin."

"Oh."

By now his lengthy strides had carried him halfway across the floor. The guests cleared a path and Walter stood ready, grinning boyishly as he opened the large wooden doors. Walter chuckled as Paul moved past him. "Don't be so impatient. You've waited this long."

Paul said something under his breath that Caroline couldn't understand and continued walking.

"How far is the cabin?" she asked.

"Too far," Paul said with a throaty chuckle. Her response to his kiss had jolted him. He'd thought he should progress to their lovemaking with less urgency—court her, let her become acquainted with him first. Yet the moment her mouth had opened to his, he'd realized there wasn't any reason to wait.

Leaning back in his arms, Caroline sighed wistfully. "Why is it dark?"

"It's October, love."

"Love?" she repeated, and sudden tears sprang to her eyes. She hadn't expected to be anyone's love—not after Larry—not for a very long time.

Paul went still. He could deal with anything but tears. "What's wrong?"

"Nothing," she murmured, sniffling. She should know not to drink champagne—especially after her aunts' special tea. Champagne always led to tears.

"Tell me." He smoothed the hair from her temple and softly kissed her there.

If he hadn't been so gentle, Caroline could have fought the unwelcome emotion. As she felt hot tears sear a path down her flushed face, she bit the corner of her bottom lip. "He left me," she whispered.

"Who?"

"Larry." She turned abruptly, wrapping her arms around Paul's neck, and sobbed into his shoulder. She wouldn't have believed she had any more tears, but her aunts' tea and the champagne had weakened her resolve to put Larry from her mind.

"You loved him?"

She nodded. "Sometimes I wonder if I'll ever stop."

The words stabbed his heart with the brutality of an ice pick. He'd known, or at least he should have known, that a woman like Caroline Myers wouldn't have agreed to marry him and live in the Alaskan wilderness without a good reason. Her letter had been so brief, so polite, unlike the others who'd tried to impress him with their wit and entice him with the promise of sexual fulfillment.

To his utter amazement, the response to his brief advertisement had been overwhelming. Dozens of letters had poured in that first week, but he hadn't bothered to read any once he'd opened Caroline's. Her picture had stopped him cold. The wheat-blond hair, the blue eyes that had spoken to him as clearly as the words of her letter. She was honest and forthright, sensual and provocative, mature and trusting. Her picture told him that, and it was confirmed by her letter. The next day he'd sent her the airplane ticket and for the past two weeks had waited in eager anticipation.

"In time, you'll learn not to love Larry," he said, kissing her temple again.

With her arms around his neck, Caroline nestled her head against his chest. "I don't know why I told you about Larry. I don't want to think about him anymore. I really don't, but he's there in my thoughts every minute."

"I'll chase him away," Paul teased.

"But how?"

"I'll find a way."

Silently they approached a log cabin and Caroline smiled at how quaint it looked with a huge set of moose antlers above the wooden door. A stepladder leaned to the right of the only window and there was a woodpile that reached up to the eaves beside it. An oblong, galvanized steel tub hung to the left of the door, along with a pair of snow-shoes.

"It's so homey. You must love it here," Caroline said as she saw the soft light in the lone window.

"I do."

"I'm sure I'll like it." She sighed deeply. She wasn't dreaming, after all— or at least not anymore.

Paul bent awkwardly to turn the door handle. The warmth that greeted them immediately made Caroline feel that this tiny cabin was the perfect place for her vacation. "It's adorable," she said, looking around.

Without question, the cabin was small—so compact that the living area and kitchen were one room. Bookcases stood beside a large potbelly stove, and a kitchen counter lined the opposite wall. A doorway led to another room that Caroline assumed would be her bedroom. Everything was spotlessly clean.

Reluctantly, Paul released her from his arms. Her feet touched the floor and she stepped back. She barely knew the man, yet she'd spilled her deepest secrets to him as though he was a lifelong friend. "Are…are you staying?"

"Would it embarrass you?"

She blinked twice. Once again they were having a conversation she didn't quite comprehend. It had to be the alcohol. Caroline shook her head to clear her muddled thoughts. "If you don't mind, I'd like to go to bed."

One side of Paul's mouth edged upward. "I was hoping you'd suggest that.

Would you feel more comfortable if I left?"

"Perhaps that would be best. I have lots of questions for you, but I'm too sleepy now. We'll talk in the morning, okay?" She took a step toward the doorway and her peripheral vision picked up the sight of the silky nightgown that had been a gift from her aunts. It was spread out across the large brass bed.

"I'll give you some time alone then," Paul said, heading for the door.

It closed after him and Caroline stood in the middle of the cabin, puzzled by the events of the day. She'd traveled thousands of miles and participated in some strange Alaskan ceremony. For a while she'd thought she was dreaming, but now realized she definitely wasn't. That meant she'd actually kissed a man whose name she hardly knew and then wept in his arms.

Moving into the single bedroom, undressing as she went, Caroline paused to admire the thick, brightly colored handmade quilt. The small lamp on the table illuminated the room and Caroline recognized her clothes hanging in an open closet beside those belonging to a man. She assumed they were Paul's. He was a gentleman, letting her use his cabin for the week and going somewhere else to sleep without complaint.

Caroline had a hazy memory of the word *wife* and wondered what *that* craziness was all about; she'd figure it out in the morning. She might even be married. A giggle escaped her as she sat on the edge of the bed. Married! Wouldn't Larry love that. Well, if she was, Paul would understand that there'd been a mistake. Her initial impression of him had been wrong. He'd intimidated her at first, but he was gentle and considerate. She'd witnessed that quality in him more than once in the past hour.

Her clothes fell to the floor as she stripped. With complete disregard, she kicked them under the bed. She'd pick them up in the morning, since she was too tired to do it now.

The sheer gown slid over her outstretched arms and down her body. The faux fur tickled her calves and Caroline smiled, recalling John's comment about how it would keep her warm. Alaskan men obviously had a sense of humor, although she hadn't been too amused at the time.

The gown *did* look like part of a wedding trousseau. Wedding? Married? She couldn't be... When she woke, they'd straighten everything out.

The bed looked soft and warm, and Caroline crawled between the sheets. Her head was cushioned by a feather pillow and her last thought before she flipped off the lamp was of the mountain she'd seen from the plane—Denali.

Somehow its magnificence comforted her and lured her into sleep.

Outside, Paul paced in front of the cabin, glancing at his watch every twenty seconds. He was cold and impatient. With the music from the reception echoing around him, he refused to return to the meeting hall. Caroline had wanted some time to prepare herself and he'd reluctantly granted her that, but he wasn't pleased. Eventually she'd learn to be less shy; there wouldn't be room for modesty when winter arrived.

Once he was sure she'd had as much time as any woman would possibly require, Paul went back into the cabin. The bedroom light was off and he could see the outline of her figure in the bed. His bed. Waiting for him. He recalled the way her body had felt against his. With vivid clarity he remembered how she'd looked at him, her blue eyes huge, when she'd suggested going to bed. Then she'd asked him if she was dreaming. The woman was drunk—drunk on her wedding night. From the day he'd received her letter, Paul had decided to wait for the rewards of marriage. Yes, he'd wait until she was ready. But, oh boy—that kiss. For a moment he'd thought she was as eager as he. He wanted their lovemaking to be slow and easy, but hadn't anticipated her effect on him. The restraint he needed not to rush to her side made him feel weak. The taste of her lips lingered on his own and left him craving more. He took a deep breath and leaned against the counter.

Hoping to gain some perspective, Paul took down the bottle of Jack Daniel's from the cupboard and poured a stiff drink. He had to think things through. He suspected she didn't believe their marriage was real, yet she had to know he'd brought her all this way for exactly that purpose. During the wedding she'd looked so confused and unsure. As her husband, he expected to claim his marital rights—only he preferred to wait until she was sober. He wanted a wife and had made that evident in his letter. This was to be a real marriage in every way, and she'd come to him on his terms. Yet he couldn't help feeling nervous.

He sat at the table and gulped down the drink, hoping to feel its numbing effect—fast. But if anything, imagining Caroline in his bed, dressed in that see-through silk gown, had the *opposite* effect on him. He'd hoped to cool his passion with sound reasoning and good whiskey, but had ended up fanning the flames.

Standing, Paul took his empty glass to the sink and saw that his hands were trembling. He felt like a coiled spring, tense, ready. Oh, yes, he was ready.

He moved into the bedroom and undressed in the dark, taking time to fold each piece of clothing and set it on the dresser. For a moment he toyed with the idea of sleeping at Walter Thundercloud's place, but quickly rejected the thought. He'd be the laughingstock of the entire community if he spent the night anywhere but with Caroline.

She was asleep, he realized from the evenness of her breathing. He was grateful for that. Much as he wanted her, he felt certain *she* wasn't ready and he needed to respect that.

The mattress dipped as he carefully slid in beside her. She sighed once and automatically rolled into his arms, nestling her head against his chest. Paul's eyes widened with the force of his resolve.

She stroked her fingertips over his lean ribs. He swallowed convulsively against the sweet torture of her touch and strengthened his self-possession by gently removing her hands. He wished she could appreciate what he was giving up....

"Love," he whispered in her ear. "Roll onto your side, okay?"

"Hmm?" Caroline was having the sweetest dream. And this time, she felt sure it really *was* a dream.

"I know you'd prefer to wait." Paul found it ironic that he was telling her this; she'd come so willingly into his arms.

"Wait?"

"Never mind," he whispered. "Just go back to sleep." Unable to resist, he kissed her forehead and shifted away from her.

Unexpectedly, the comforting, irresistible warmth beside her moved and Caroline edged closer to it. With a sigh of longing, she buried her face in the hollow of his neck.

"Caroline, please, this is difficult

enough," he whispered, inhaling harshly. She flattened her hand against his abdomen and slowly brushed her lips over his.

With every muscle, Paul struggled for control. Seconds later, he was lost—irrevocably and completely lost. Their kiss was unlike any he'd ever experienced.... But Paul was the one to break contact, twisting so that he lay on his back. His control, such as it was, seemed to be slipping fast; another minute and he wouldn't have been able to stop.

Caroline felt unbearably hot, as if she was sitting directly in front of a fireplace. The thought was so illogical—she was in bed, wasn't she?—that she bolted upright, giggling, and tossed the blankets aside. She fell back onto the pillow and raised her hands above her head, intertwining her fingers. The ceiling was spinning around and around. In an effort to block out the dizzying sight, she closed her eyes and sought anew the security of the dream.

Again Paul tried to move away from her but Caroline wanted him close. She couldn't understand why he kept leaving her. If he was part of her dream, the least he could do was stick around! She reached for him, locking her arms around his neck, kissing him.

"Caroline, stop it!"

"Why?"

"Because you're drunk," he hissed.

She giggled. "I know." Her fingers roamed over his shoulders. "Please kiss me again. Has anyone ever told you that you're a great kisser?"

"I can't kiss you." *And remain sane,* he added silently.

"But I *want* you to." She sounded like a whiny child and that shocked her. "Oh, never mind, I wouldn't kiss me either." With that she let out a noisy yawn and rested her cheek against his chest.

"You have nice skin," she murmured before closing her eyes.

"You do, too," he whispered, and slid his hand down the length of her spine. "Very nice."

"Are you sure you don't want to kiss me?"

Paul groaned. His nobility had limitations, and he wasn't going to be able to hold off much longer if she asked him to kiss her every ten seconds.

"Good night, love," he whispered, hoping his voice had the ring of finality. He kissed the crown of her head and continued to hold her close, almost savoring the sweet torture.

Caroline smiled, content. Just before she gave in to the irrepressible urge to sleep, she felt his kiss, and prayed that all her dreams would be this real and this exciting.

Snuggling closer to the warm body at her side, Caroline woke slowly. Her first conscious thought was that her head ached. It more than ached; it throbbed with each pulse and every sluggish heartbeat as her memory returned, muddled and confused. She rolled onto her back, holding the sides of her head, and groaned aloud. She was in bed with a man she barely knew. Unfortunately, he appeared to be well acquainted with her. Extremely well acquainted. Her first inclination was to kick him out of the bed. He'd taken advantage of her inebriated state, and she bit back bitter words as a flush of embarrassment burned her cheeks.

Opening her eyes was an impossible task. She couldn't face the man.

"Good morning," the deep male voice purred.

"It…wasn't a dream, was it?" she asked in a tone that was faint and apprehensive.

Paul chuckled. "You mean you honestly don't remember anything?"

"Some." She kept her eyes pinched shut, too mortified to look at him.

"Do you remember the part about us getting married?"

Caroline blinked. "I'm not sure."

"In case you don't, I suppose I should introduce myself. I'm Paul Trevor, your husband."

Three

"Then it *was* real!" Still holding her head, Caroline struggled to a sitting position. Gradually her eyes opened and she glared down at the bearded man beside her.

Paul was lying on his side, watching her with an amused grin. He rose up on his elbow and shook his head. "I can't believe you didn't expect to be married."

She felt as though the heat in her face was enough to keep the cabin warm all winter. "I knew at the time you...you weren't completely a dream." She had to be honest, even at the expense of her stubborn pride.

"We're married, love."

"Stop calling me your love! I am not your love, or any other man's. And we've certainly got to do something about annulling this…this marriage." She winced at the flash of pain that shot through her head.

"If you'd rather I didn't call you love, I won't."

"Call me Caroline or Ms. Myers, anything but your love."

"I *am* your husband."

"Will you stop saying that?"

"I have the paperwork to prove it."

Caroline tucked the blankets under her arms and scowled at him with all the fury she could muster. "Then I challenge you to produce them."

"As you wish." He threw aside the

blankets and climbed out of bed, standing only partially clothed before her.

Caroline looked away. "I would really appreciate it if you'd put something on."

"Why?" He sent a questioning glance over his shoulder.

The red flush seeped down to her neck and she swallowed convulsively. "Just do it.... Please."

Chuckling again, Paul withdrew a slip of paper from his shirt pocket. "Here," he said, handing it to her.

Caroline grabbed it and quickly unfolded it, then scanned the contents. The document looked official and her name was signed at the bottom, although she barely recognized the signature as her own. Vaguely she remembered Paul having her sign some papers when they'd entered the meeting hall. She'd been so bemused she'd thought it had to do with registering a guest.

"I signed first," Paul explained, "and gave you the pen."

"Yes…but at the time I assumed it was something all tourists did." It sounded so ridiculous now that she wanted to weep at her own stupidity. "The party yesterday was our wedding reception, wasn't it?"

"Yes."

Caroline shook her head. "I…I thought Gold River got so few tourists that they greeted everyone like that."

"Caroline, you're not making any sense."

"*I'm* not?" she shouted, then winced. "You should look at it from my point of view."

"But you agreed to marry me weeks ago."

"I most certainly did not!"

"I have the letter."

"Now that I'd like to see. I may not have been in full control of my wits yesterday, but I know for a fact I'd never heard of you until…" The words died on her lips. "My aunts—my romantic, idealistic, scheming aunts…they couldn't have. They wouldn't…"

Paul regarded her suspiciously. "What aunts?"

"Mine. Just get the letter and p-please…" she stammered, "please put something on. This is all extremely embarrassing."

Grumbling under his breath, Paul reached for his pants and pulled them on, snapping them at the waist. Next he unfolded his shirt and slipped his arms inside the long sleeves, but he left it unbuttoned. "There. Are you satisfied?"

"Somewhat." Speaking of clothes reminded Caroline of her own skimpy state of dress. When Paul's back was turned, she scurried to the very edge of the mattress in a frantic search for her cords and sweater. She remembered undressing, but she couldn't recall where she'd put her things.

Stretching down as far as possible, Caroline made a wide sweep under the bed and managed to retrieve her sweater. Fearing Paul would be back at any minute, she slid her arms into the bulky sleeves and yanked it over her head. As she shook her hair free of the confining collar, Caroline came eye to eye with Paul.

He stood over her, his grin slightly off center. "Just give me that letter," Caroline demanded.

"Would you like me to read it to you?"

"No." She grabbed for it, but he held it just out of her reach. "I don't appreciate these sophomoric games, Paul Trevor."

"Go ahead and read it for yourself while I fix us something to eat."

"I'm not hungry," she announced

sharply, jerking the envelope from his hand. Food was the last thing on her mind.

Humming as though he didn't have a care in the world, Paul left the bedroom while Caroline's eyes narrowed on his back. How dare he act so...so unruffled by this unexpected turn of events.

The instant Paul was out of sight, Caroline tore into the letter. The creases were well worn and with a mild attack of guilt she realized he must have read the neatly typed page repeatedly.

Dear Paul,
My name is Caroline Myers and I'm responding to your advertisement in the *Seattle Post-Intelligencer.* I am seeking a husband to love. My picture is enclosed, but I'm actually more attractive in person. That isn't to say, however, that I'm the least bit vain. I enjoy fish-

ing and hiking and Scrabble and other games of skill. Since I am the last of the Ezra Myers family left in the Northwest, I am interested in having children. I'm a nurse currently employed by Dr. Kenneth James, but can leave my employment on two weeks' notice. I look forward to hearing from you.

Most sincerely,

The evenly shaped letters of her name were penned at the bottom of the page in what Caroline recognized as her Aunt Mabel's handwriting.

With sober thoughts, Caroline dressed, then joined Paul in the kitchen. He pulled out a chair and handed her a cup of coffee.

She laid the letter on the table. "I didn't write this."

"I figured that might've been the case."

Her face flushed, she wondered just what had happened after the ceremony. Surely she'd remember something as important as that. "I have these two elderly aunts…." Caroline hedged, not knowing where exactly to start her explanation.

"So I gathered." He pulled out the chair across from her and placed his elbows on the table. "They answered my advertisement?"

"Apparently so."

"How'd they convince you to marry me?"

"That's just it…. They didn't." Caroline dumped a tablespoon of sugar into the coffee and stirred it several times.

"Then why did you go through with it?"

"I…wasn't myself yesterday. I…I didn't fully realize what was happening." She knew how ridiculous that sounded and hurried to explain. "You see, Aunt Mabel and Aunt Ethel—they're really my great-aunts, but I've always called them Aunt—anyway, they told me they were giving me a trip to Alaska."

"Why?"

She wasn't sure how much she wanted to reveal. She understood the reason her two scheming aunts had answered Paul's ad. They'd been worried about her after the breakup with Larry. The question was: How was she going to untangle herself from this unfortunate set of circumstances? "The purpose for my agreeing to come to Alaska isn't important," she told him stiffly.

"Not too many people visit Alaska on the brink of winter," he said.

She wished he'd stop arguing with her. Keeping her composure under these conditions was difficult enough.

"Was it because of Larry?"

Caroline felt her blood run cold. "They told you about Larry?"

"No, you did."

"I did!" She opened her eyes wide, then quickly lowered them. "Is there anything I didn't tell you?"

"I imagine there's quite a bit." He paused to drink his coffee. "Please go on. I'm curious to hear how you got yourself into this predicament."

"Well, Aunt Mabel and Aunt Ethel insisted I take this trip. I'd never been to Alaska and they kept telling me how beautiful it is. I didn't know how they could afford it, but—"

"They didn't."

"What do you mean?" She held the mug with both hands. This was getting more complicated by the minute.

"I paid for it."

"Terrific," she groaned. She'd need to repay him for that and God only knew what else.

She paused for a sip of coffee and continued her explanation. "Then John Morrison met me in Fairbanks and the ride to Gold River got a bit rugged, so I drank the thermos of tea my aunts sent along."

"Tea?"

"Not regular tea," Caroline corrected. "My aunts have a special brew—their father passed the recipe to them."

"I see." One corner of his lip curved upward as he made an obvious—but futile— effort to contain his smile.

Caroline wasn't fooled. "Would you stop looking amused? We're in one heck of a mess here."

"We are?" He cocked an eyebrow expressively. "We're married, Caroline, and the ceremony is as legal as it gets. We stood before God, with the whole village as witness."

"But you don't honestly expect me to

honor those vows.... You can't be that unreasonable."

"We're married."

"It was a mistake!"

"Not as far as I'm concerned."

"I'll have it annulled," she threatened.

His grin was wide and cynical. "After last night?"

Her cheeks flamed even hotter. So something *had* happened. "All right," she said tightly, "we'll get a divorce."

"There will be no divorce."

Caroline placed her mug on the table. "You can't be serious! I have no intention of staying married to you. Good heavens, I don't even *know* you."

"You'll have plenty of time for that later."

"Later? Are you nuts? I'm not staying here a second longer than necessary. There's been a terrible mistake and I want out before something else happens."

"And I say we make the best of the situation."

"Just how do you propose we do that?"

"Stay married."

"You're crazy." She stood up so abruptly that the chair went crashing to the floor. "Let's talk about this in a logical fashion."

"The deed is done." In Paul's opinion, there was nothing to discuss; she was here in his home and they were legally married.

"Deed," Caroline echoed, feeling slightly sick to her stomach. "Then we…I mean, last night, you and I… we…?" Her eyes implored him to tell her what they'd done.

Paul yearned to assure her they'd shared only a few kisses, but the instant he told her that nothing—well, almost nothing—had happened, she'd bolt. "Caroline, listen to me. It's too late for argument."

"Not from my point of view." Her arms were wrapped around her stomach as she paced the floor. "I want out of here and I want out now."

Paul shrugged. "That's unfortunate because you're staying."

"You can't force me!"

His frustration was quickly mounting. "Would you give us a chance? I'll admit we're getting off to a shaky start, but things will work out."

"Work out!" she cried. "I'm married to a man whose face I can't even see."

Paul ran his hand over the neatly trimmed beard. "It's winter and my beard's there to protect my face from the cold. I won't shave until spring."

"I…I don't know you," she said again.

"I wouldn't say that."

"Will you stop bringing up the subject of last night?"

Caroline was surprised by Paul's low chuckle. "*Now* what's so funny?" she asked.

"You're a passionate woman, Mrs. Trevor. If it's this good between us at the beginning, can you imagine how fantastic it'll be when we know each other better?"

"Stop it!" Furious, she stalked across the room and stood in front of the window. A thin layer of snow covered the ground and in the distance Caroline could see the form of a small plane against the blue sky. Her heart rate soared as she contemplated her means of escape. If the plane landed in Gold River, maybe she could sneak out before Paul discovered she was missing.

"Caroline?"

She turned back to him. "Were you so desperate for a wife that you had to advertise? That doesn't say a whole lot about your sterling character."

"There are very few opportunities in Alaska, love. I don't often get into Fairbanks."

"I already asked you not to call me that."

"I apologize."

He didn't look the least bit contrite and his attitude infuriated her further. "Why did you choose *me?* You must've received more than one response."

"I received...several." *Hundreds, if the truth be known.* "I chose you because I liked your eyes."

"Wonderful!" She threw her hands in the air.

"But your aunts were right—you are more attractive in person."

Caroline couldn't believe what she was hearing. Paul Trevor apparently expected her to honor her vows and live here on this chunk of ice. She was growing increasingly frantic. "I...have disgusting habits. Within a week you'll be ready to toss me to the wolves."

"There isn't anything we won't be able to work out."

"Paul, please, look at it from my perspective." Her eyes pleaded with him.

Paul struggled with the effect they had on him. It was difficult to refuse her anything, but the matter of their marriage was something on which he couldn't compromise. "We'll discuss it later," he told her stiffly and turned away. "I've got to get to the station."

"What station?"

"The pump station by the pipeline."

"Oh. John mentioned it." Already her mind was scheming. She'd let him go and pray that the plane circling overhead would land. If it did, she could convince the pilot to get her out of Gold River before Paul even knew she was gone.

"I won't be more than an hour or two."

"All right." She slowly rubbed the palms of her hands together. "And when you get back, I'm sure we'll be able to reach some agreement. I might even be willing to stay."

Paul eyed her suspiciously, not trusting this sudden change of heart. While he shrugged into his coat, he said, "I want your word, Caroline, that you'll remain in the cabin."

"Here? In this cabin?"

"Your word of honor."

Caroline swallowed uncomfortably; she hated lying. Normally she spokc the truth even to her own detriment. "All right," she muttered, childishly crossing her fingers behind her back. "I'll stay here."

"I have your word?"

"Yes." Without flinching, her eyes met his.

"I won't be long." His hand was on the doorknob.

"Take your time." The plane was landing; she could hear it in the distance. "While you're gone, I'll find my way around the kitchen," she said brightly. "By the time you return, I'll have lunch ready."

Again Paul eyed her doubtfully. She sounded much too eager for him to leave, but he didn't have time to worry now. Giving her a few hours alone was probably for the best. She'd promised to stay and he had no choice but to trust her. He was already an hour late. Walter had said he'd stand in for him, but Paul had refused. The station was his responsibility.

The second the door closed after Paul, Caroline dashed into the bedroom and jerked her clothes off the hangers, stuffing them back inside her suitcase. With a sense of guilt, she left the winter gear that Paul had purchased on her behalf. He'd gone to a great deal of trouble and expense for her, but she couldn't be blamed for that.

A quick check at the door revealed that Paul was nowhere in sight. She breathed a bit easier and walked cautiously outside. Although the day was clear, the cold cut straight through her thin jacket.

A couple of Athabascan women passed Caroline and smiled shyly, their eyes curious. She returned their silent greeting and experienced a twinge of remorse at this regrettable subterfuge. If he'd been more reasonable, she wouldn't have had to do something so drastic.

The plane was taxiing to a stop at the airstrip where she'd been dropped off less than twenty-four hours earlier.

Caroline watched from the center of town as the pilot handed down several plywood crates. A few minutes later, the dogsleds and snowmobiles arrived.

"Hi." She stepped forward, her calm smile concealing her anxiety.

The tall burly man seemed surprised to see her. "Hello."

"I'm Caroline Myers." She extended her hand for him to shake and prayed he wouldn't detect her nervousness.

"Burt Manners. What can I do for you?"

"I need a ride to Fairbanks," she said quickly. "Is there any way you could fly me there?"

"Sorry, lady, I'm headed in the opposite direction."

"Where?" She'd go anyplace as long as it was away from Gold River and Paul.

"Near Circle Hot Springs."

"That's fine. I'll go there first, just so it's understood that you can fly me to Fairbanks afterward."

"Lady, I've already got a full load. Besides, you don't want to travel to Circle Hot Springs. It's no place for a lady this time of year."

"I don't care. Honest."

"There isn't any room." He started to turn away from her.

"There must be *some* space available. You just unloaded those crates. Please." Caroline hated the whiny sound of her voice, but she was desperate. The sooner she escaped, the better.

"Is that the warmest coat you've got?"

He was looking for excuses and Caroline knew it. "No. I've got another coat. Can I come?"

"I don't know...." Still, he hesitated.

"I'll pay you double your normal fee," Caroline said, placing her hand on his forearm. "I *have* to get to Fairbanks."

"Okay, okay." Burt rubbed his neck. "Why do I feel I'm going to regret this?"

Caroline hardly heard him as she made a sharp turn and scurried across the snow toward the cabin. "I'll be right back. Don't leave without me."

She got to the cabin breathless with excitement and relief, and hurried into the bedroom. Taking the coat Paul had purchased for her went against all her instincts, but she'd repay him later, she rationalized, once she was safely back in Seattle. To ease her conscience, she quickly scribbled an IOU and left it on the kitchen table, where he was sure to find it, along with a note apologizing for the lie. Her suitcase stood just inside the doorway. She reached for it with one hand and her purse with the other.

The pilot was waiting for her when she returned and she climbed aboard, feeling jubilant. Getting away from Paul had been much easier than she'd expected. Of course he could follow her, but that was doubtful unless he had a plane, and she didn't see a hangar anywhere.

As Burt had explained, the seating was cramped.

He talked little on the short trip, which suited Caroline just fine. She didn't have a whole lot to say herself.

The landing strip at Circle Hot Springs looked even more unreliable than the one at Gold River. Caroline felt her stomach pitch wildly when the Cessna's wheels slammed against the frozen ground, but she managed to conceal her alarm.

They were met by a group of four hunters who unloaded the plane, delivering the gear to a huge hunting lodge. When they'd finished, one of the men brought out a bottle of whiskey and passed it around. The largest hunter, a man called Sam, offered the bottle to Caroline.

"No, thanks," she said shaking her head. "I prefer to drink mine from a glass." Burt had said that Circle Hot

Springs wasn't any place for a lady, but she'd assumed he'd been concerned about the climate.

"Hey, guys, we've got a classy dame with us." Sam laughed gruffly and handed her the bottle. "Take a drink," he ordered.

Fear sent chills racing up and down her spine as Caroline looked frantically at Burt. "I said no, thank you."

"Lay off, you guys," Burt called. "She doesn't have to drink if she doesn't want to."

An hour later, Caroline was convinced she'd made a horrible mistake. The men sat around drinking and telling dirty jokes that were followed by smutty songs and laughter. Their conversation, or at least what she could hear of it, was filled with innuendo. The more she ignored them, the more they seemed to focus on her.

While the men were engaged in a discussion about the next day's plans, Caroline crept close to Burt's side, doing everything possible to remove attention from herself.

"You okay?" Burt muttered.

"Fine," she lied. "When do we leave for Fairbanks?"

He gave her an odd look. "Not until tomorrow morning."

"Tomorrow morning? That long?" She gulped. What had she gotten herself into now?

"Hey, lady, you asked for this."

"Right." She'd left the frying pan and landed directly in the hot coals of the fire. "I'll be ready first thing in the morning." Although it was the middle of the afternoon, the skies were already beginning to darken.

The hunting lodge had a large living room with a mammoth fireplace. The proprietor/guide appeared and introduced himself, then brought out another bottle of whiskey to welcome his latest guests. Caroline refused a drink and inquired politely about renting a room for the night.

"Sorry, honey, we're full up."

His eyes were twinkling and Caroline didn't believe him.

"You can stay with me," Sam offered.

"No, thanks."

"Polite little thing, ain't you?" Sam slipped his arm around her shoulders and squeezed hard. The smell of alcohol on his breath nearly bowled her over. "The boys and me came here for some fun and we're real glad you decided to join us."

"I'm just passing through on my way to Fairbanks," she explained lamely. She cast a pleading glance at Burt, but he was talking to another of the men and didn't notice her. She groaned inwardly when she saw the glass of amber liquid in his hand.

"Like I said, we came into Circle Hot Springs for a little fun," Sam told her, slurring his words. "You knew that when you insisted on flying here, I'll bet." Again he gave her shoulders a rough squeeze.

Caroline felt as if her vocal cords had frozen with fear. As the evening progressed, things went from bad to worse. After the men had eaten, they grew louder and even more boisterous. Burt had started drinking and from the looks he was giving her, Caroline wondered just how much protection he'd be if worse came to worst. Judging by the way he was staring at her, Caroline realized he wouldn't be much help against the burly men.

Sam polished off his glass of whiskey and rubbed the back of his hand across his mouth. "I don't know about the rest of you yahoos," he shouted, "but I'm game for some entertainment."

"What do you have in mind?"

"Burt brought it for us. Ain't that right, little lady?"

Once again Caroline's eyes pleaded with Burt, but he ignored her silent petition. "I…I didn't say anything like that, but…but I think you should know, I'm not much of a singer."

The men broke into loud guffaws.

"I can dance a little," she offered, hoping to delay any arguments and discover a means of escape. Her heart felt as though it were refusing to cooperate with her lungs. She'd never been so scared in her life.

"Let her dance."

The whiskey bottle was passed from one member of the party to the next as Caroline stood and edged to the front door. If she could break free, she might be able to locate another cabin to spend the night. Someplace warm and safe.

"I'll…need some music." She recognized her mistake when two of the men broke into a melody associated with strippers.

"Dance," Sam called, clapping his hands.

"Sure." Caroline was close to tears of anger and frustration. Swinging her hands at her sides, she did a shuffle she'd learned in tap dance class in the fifth grade.

The men booed.

She sent them a feeble smile and stopped. "I guess I'm not much of a dancer, either."

"Try harder," someone shouted, and they all laughed again.

The log door swung open and a cold north wind caused the roaring fire to flicker. A man entered, his head covered with a hood. He flipped it back and stared at Caroline.

"Paul!" She'd never been so glad to

see anyone in her life. She wanted to weep with relief.

"What's going on here?" he said gruffly.

"We're just havin' a little fun," Burt said, lurching to his feet. "Do you know the lady?"

Paul looked directly at Caroline and slowly shook his head. "Nope. Never seen her before in my life."

Four

Caroline stared with utter astonishment as Paul took a seat with the other men, removing his parka and setting it aside. Someone passed him a drink, which he quickly downed. Not once did he glance in her direction.

"Well," he said after a moment, "what's stopping you? Dance."

"Dance?" Caroline repeated.

"Dance!" all the men shouted simultaneously.

"And no more little-girl stuff, either."

Caroline's anger simmered just below

the surface. Couldn't Paul see that she was up to her neck in trouble? The least he could do was rescue her. All morning he'd kept saying he was her husband and nothing she could do would change that. Well, good grief, if she'd ever needed a husband it was now. Instead, he appeared to find her predicament humorous. Well, she'd show him!

Heaving a deep sigh, she resumed her soft-shoe shuffle, swinging her arms at her sides. She really did need music and if the men weren't going to provide it, she'd make her own. Perhaps because of the snow outside, all she could think of was Christmas songs. "Jingle bell, jingle bell, jingle bell rock…" she bellowed out.

The only one she seemed to amuse was Paul, but his laugh could be better described as a snicker. Although Caroline made a point of not looking at him, she could feel the heat of his anger. All right, so she'd lied. And she'd taken the coat. She did intend to pay him for it, plus what he'd spent on her airplane fare.

The men were booing her efforts again.

"I told you, none of that kid stuff," Sam shouted, his voice even more slurred. "You're supposed to *entertain* us."

As much as she hated to reveal her fright, Caroline stopped and she silently begged Paul for help. Again he ignored her.

"Take your clothes off," Sam called out. "That's what we want."

"Paul?" she whispered, and her voice trembled. "Please." When she saw him clench his fists, she knew she'd won.

"All right, guys," he said, agilely rising to his feet. "The game's over. I'd like you to meet my wife."

"Your wife!" In a rush, Burt Manners

jumped from his sitting position. "Hey, buddy, I swear I had no idea."

"Wait a minute!" Sam burst out. "You said you didn't know her and—"

"Don't worry about it," Paul cut in.

"She came to me begging to leave Gold River. I told her Circle Hot Springs was no place for a lady, but she insisted."

Paul's mouth thinned. "I know."

"You need me to fly you back to Gold River?" Burt asked eagerly.

"No, thanks, I've got someone waiting."

"You do?" Caroline was so relieved, she felt faint. Another minute of this horrible tension would have been unbearable. The men were looking at her as though she was some cheat who'd swindled them out of an evening's fun and games. And from the way Paul kept avoiding eye contact, she wondered what he'd say once they were alone.

She'd gone from the frying pan into the fire and then back to the frying pan.

Burt stepped out of the hunting lodge with them to unload Caroline's suitcase from his plane. With every step, he continued to apologize until Caroline wanted to scream. Paul knew she'd practically begged the other man to take her away from Gold River. He didn't need to hear it over and over again.

"Fact is," Burt said, standing beside his Cessna, his expression uneasy, "I didn't hear you were married. If I'd known she was your wife, I never would've taken her."

Paul offered no excuse for her behavior. He was so silent and so furious that Caroline thought he might explode any minute. Without a word, he escorted her to the waiting plane and helped her inside, every movement that of a perfect gentleman. But she had no doubt whatsoever that he was enraged.

Once aboard the plane, Caroline smiled faintly at the pilot and slipped into her seat. No sooner had she buckled her safety belt than the engines roared to life and the Cessna taxied away.

Paul was quiet for the entire flight. By the time they circled Gold River, Caroline was weak with dread—and guilt. She'd lied to Paul, stolen from him and embarrassed him in front of his friends. Maybe he'd be so glad to get rid of her that he'd give her the divorce. Maybe this whole fiasco could be annulled. Oh heavens, why wouldn't he tell her what had happened last night? She rubbed her temples, trying to recall the events following her arrival. She remembered him kissing her and how good it felt, but beyond that her memory was a blur.

When the plane approached the runway, Caroline closed her eyes. The sensation of the frozen tundra rising to meet the small aircraft made her dizzy.

The Cessna jerked hard once, then again, and for a moment Caroline was sure they were going to crash. A fitting end to her day, she thought gloomily— death. She swallowed a cry of alarm and looked frantically at Paul, who was seated beside her. His face was void of expression, as though such a bumpy landing was nothing out of the ordinary. They eased to a stop, and Caroline sagged against the back of the seat, breathless with relief.

Walter was standing with a team of huskies to meet them. His ageless eyes hardened when he caught a glimpse of Caroline, and his angry glare could have split a rock.

"Could you see that Bill has a hot meal and place to spend the night?" Paul asked his friend, apparently referring to the pilot.

"Sure thing."

Once inside the cabin, Caroline

turned her back to the woodstove and waited. Paul walked past her, carrying her suitcase into the bedroom.

Caroline removed her parka and hung it beside Paul's. The cabin was warm and cozy, some kind of stew was simmering on top of the stove and the enticing smell was enough to make Caroline feel limp. She hadn't eaten all day.

Still, Paul didn't speak and she waited another minute before she broached a conversation.

"Okay, I'm ready," she said when she couldn't stand it any longer.

"Ready for what?"

"For whatever you're going to say or do to me."

"I'm not going to say or do anything."

"Nothing?" Caroline uttered in stunned disbelief.

Paul crossed the tiny kitchen and took two bowls from the cupboard.

"But I lied to you."

His eyes narrowed. "I know."

"And I stole the coat."

He nodded.

"And…" Her voice trembled. "I made a fool out of us both."

Paul lifted the lid of the cast iron kettle, filled each bowl to the top with stew and brought them to the table.

Caroline gripped the back of the kitchen chair. "You must be furious with me."

"I am."

"Then don't you think you should divorce me? I mean—it's obvious I'm not the woman you want. If I were you, I'd be willing to admit I made a bad choice and go from there." She eyed him hopefully.

He sat down, unfolded his napkin and laid it across his lap. "There will be no divorce."

"But I don't *want* to be married! I—"

"The deed is done."

"What deed?" she screamed. If she'd had a wedding night, a *real* wedding night, surely she'd remember it.

"We're legally married," hc said calmly, reaching for his spoon. "Now sit down and eat."

"No." Stubbornly, she crossed her arms over her chest.

"Fine. Then don't eat."

Caroline glanced at the steaming bowl of stew. Her mouth bcgan to water and she angrily pulled out the chair. "All right, I'll eat," she murmured, "but I'm doing it under protest." She dipped her spoon into the thick mixture.

"I can tell," Paul said.

When they'd finished, it was Paul who cleared the table and washed the dishes. Wordlessly, Caroline found a dish towel and dried them, replacing the bowls in the overhead cupboard. Her mind was spinning with possible topics of conversation, all of which led to one central issue: their marriage. She prayed she'd find a way of getting him to listen to reason.

An hour after dinner, Paul turned off the lights in the living room and moved into the bedroom. Caroline could either follow him or be left standing alone in the dark. She didn't even consider turning on the lights again.

The instant her gaze fell on the bed, Caroline knew she could delay no longer. "Paul, listen to me—there's been a terrible mistake."

"There was no mistake," he countered, starting to unbutton his shirt.

Briefly, Caroline recalled running her fingers down his chest. She felt the blood drain from her face and turned away in an effort not to look at him. If there was anything else to remember, she didn't want to do it now. "The mistake wasn't yours, I'll admit that. But you must understand that I didn't know anything about the wedding."

"We've already been through this and no amount of talk is going to change what happened. We're married, and as far as I'm concerned that's how we're going to stay."

"But I don't want to be married," she wailed.

Paul heaved a disgusted sigh. "Would it make any difference if I was your beloved Larry?"

"Yes," she cried, then quickly changed her mind. "No, it wouldn't. Oh hell, I don't know."

"The subject is closed," Paul said forcefully. "We won't discuss it again."

"But we have to."

From behind her, Caroline heard Paul throw back the covers and climb into bed. Slowly, she turned, feeling more unhappy and depressed than at any other time in her life.

"Surely you don't believe I'm going to sleep with you?"

"You're my wife, Caroline."

"But…"

"Why do you insist on arguing? We're married. You're my wife and I want you to sleep in my bed."

"I won't."

"Fine," he grumbled. "Sleep on the floor. When you get cold enough you'll come to bed." With that, he rolled onto his side and flipped off the light, once again leaving Caroline in the dark. She remained where she was for a long moment, indecisive, exhausted, bewildered.

"Paul?"

"Hmm?"

"If I… If I come to bed, will you promise not to touch me?"

Silence. Finally he said, "After the stunt you pulled today, I doubt that I could."

Caroline supposed she should've been relieved, but she wasn't. Slowly, she undressed and climbed under the blankets. She shivered once and curled up tightly. As weary as she was, she'd expected to fall directly into a deep sleep, but she didn't. In fact, a half hour later, she lay wide awake, surprisingly warm and cozy.

"Paul?" she whispered.

"What?"

She bit her bottom lip to hold back the tears. "I'm sorry about today."

"I know."

"Under normal conditions, I would never have done anything so stupid."

"I know that, too."

"Do you know everything?" she snapped.

"No."

"I'm glad to hear it."

Another five minutes passed. "Paul?"

"What is it now?"

"Good night."

"Good night, love." She could hear the relief in his voice and her eyes drifted shut.

The next thing Caroline knew, Paul was leaning over her, gently shaking her awake.

"Caroline, it's morning."

Her eyes flew open in alarm and she brushed the hair from her face. "What time is it?"

"Five o'clock. You'll need to get up and dressed. There's coffee on the dresser for you."

Maybe he'd relented and had accepted the impossibility of their circumstances. She struggled into a sitting position, her eyes finding his. "Up and dressed? Why?" she asked, hoping he'd decided to send her back to Seattle.

"You're coming with me."

"Where?"

"To the pump station."

Her spirits sagged. "But why? I don't know anything about—"

"I can't trust you. So I don't have any choice but to bring you with me."

"I'm not going to run away again. I promise."

"You promised before. Now get up."

"But, Paul, I won't—"

"I don't have time to argue with you. Either you do as I say or I'll take you with me dressed as you are."

Caroline didn't doubt him for a second. "Aye, aye, commander," she said and gave him a mocking salute. Furious, she threw back the sheets and reached for her clothes.

Caroline had never spent a more boring morning in her life. Paul sat her down in a chair and left her to twiddle her thumbs for what seemed like hours. After the first thirty minutes, she toyed with the idea of walking back to the cabin, which she found preferable to sitting in a chair, a punishment more befitting a badly behaved child. However, she quickly discarded that idea. All she needed was to have Paul return to find her gone. If he was furious with her after yesterday, it would be nothing compared to his anger if she pulled the same trick twice. So, although she was bored senseless, Caroline stayed exactly where she was.

Paul returned and she brightened, pleased to have some human contact. But to her dismay, he walked directly past her to another desk and took out a huge ledger, proceeding to record data.

"Paul?"

"Shh."

She pressed her lips together so hard they hurt.

He lifted his head when he'd finished and looked at her expectantly. "You wanted something?"

"I want to go back to the cabin."

"No."

"After what happened yesterday, you can't believe I'll try to get away again." He returned to his work and refused to look at her, ostensibly studying his ledger. Caroline's blood was close to the boiling point. "What are you going to do? Keep me with you twenty-four hours a day?"

"You gave me no option."

"You *can't* be serious. I'm not going to run away." She pointed to the front door. "There are crazy people out there."

He didn't respond.

"Paul, please, I'll go out of my mind with nothing to do."

"Get a book and read." His response was as uncaring as the arctic wind that howled outside the door.

"Oh, I see," she said in a high-pitched, emotional voice. "This is to be my punishment. Not only are you going to keep me as your prisoner, but I have to suffer your company as well. How long?"

"How long what?" With deliberate care, he set his pen aside.

"How long before you learn to trust me? A week? Ten days? A month?"

"I can't answer that. It depends on you."

She flew to her feet, her fists clenched. "Well then, you'd be wise never to leave me alone, because the minute I get a chance, I'm high-tailing it out of here. Somehow or other, I'll find a way to escape. You can't keep a person against his or her will. This is the United States of America and kidnapping is against the law."

"I didn't kidnap you, I married you."

"Well, then, you're the worst possible husband a woman could have. I refuse to be your wife, no matter what some piece of paper says." She waited for him to argue with her and when he didn't, she continued her tirade. "Not only that... You've got to be the most stubborn man I've ever met. Stubborn and unreasonable and...and...chauvinistic to boot!"

Paul nodded. "I know. But given time, you'll learn to love me."

"Never," Caroline vowed. "Not while I live and breathe."

"We'll see."

He sounded so sure of himself, so confident, that she wanted to throttle him. Drained, she sank back into her chair. To her horror, tears filled her eyes and fell hot against her cheeks. She wiped them aside and sniffled loudly to hold back the flood. "Paul," she cried softly. "I just want to go home. Please."

His mouth grew hard and inflexible. "You are home. The sooner you accept that, the better for both of us."

With that, Caroline buried her face in her hands and wept until there were no tears left. Her eyes burned and her throat ached.

Paul felt the weight of Denali pressing against his back, and prayed he was doing the right thing. He could deal with her harangues, even her feisty anger, but her tears were another matter. They brought all his doubts to the surface. A month—he'd promised himself a month. If things hadn't improved by the end of October, he'd send her back to Seattle. Looking at her now, bent over, weeping as though she hadn't a friend in the world, he felt guilt—and an overwhelming compassion. It would be so easy to love her. She had spunk and character and was more woman than he'd ever dreamed he'd find. He knew in his heart that this really could work, that this marriage could be genuine and happy. He knew because— except for one occasion—his instincts hadn't steered him wrong yet and where

there was such intense attraction between a man and a woman, there was
a chance for lasting love.

By midafternoon, Caroline had read
one adventure novel, written her two
maiden aunts a scathing letter, destroyed that, and had drawn several pic-
tures of a distorted Paul with a knife
through his heart. She couldn't help it;
after eight hours of complete monotony,
she felt murderous.

Toward evening, Paul handed Caroline her parka. "Are you ready to go
back to the cabin?"

Was she ever! But she had no intention of letting him know that. With a
regal tilt of her chin, she reached for her
jacket and slipped her arms inside the
thick sleeves. She hadn't spoken a word
to Paul in hours and he hadn't had the
decency to reveal the least bit of concern. Well, she could hold out longer
than he could. By the time she returned

to Seattle, he'd be so glad to be rid of her, he'd give her the divorce without even arguing.

More snow had fallen during the day, and although the cabin was only a short distance from the pumping station, they needed snowshoes to trek their way back. It was the first time that Caroline had ever worn them, and she was forced to squelch her natural delight.

Again, dinner had been left on the stove. Tonight it was a roast with onions, potatoes and carrots simmered in the gravy. Caroline wondered who did the cooking, but she refused to ask Paul a thing. And she was hungry; lunch had consisted of a peanut butter sandwich many hours before.

As he had the previous night, Paul placed the silverware on the table and brought their meal from the stove. More than once Caroline felt his gaze on her, but she was determined not to utter a word.

"I must admit," Paul said halfway through their dinner, "that I prefer the silence to your constant badgering."

"Badgering!" Caroline shrieked. "I do not badger. All I want is an end to this despicable marriage."

Paul grinned boyishly. "Has anyone told you how beautiful your eyes are?"

Caroline pressed her lips together and stabbed her meat with unnecessary force. "I wish that was your heart. Oops, my mistake. You don't have one."

Paul laughed outright at that. "But I do, love," he said a few minutes later. "And it belongs to you."

"I don't want it." She struggled to hold back tears of frustration "Didn't you say you'd received lots of letters in response to your ad? Those women all *wanted* to be your wife. Let me go, Paul. Please let me go. I'll repay you the money you've already spent. I swear I will."

He shook his head. "I refuse to discuss the matter again." Until the end of the month, he added to himself, hoping that by then there'd be nothing to discuss.

"Yes, your Majesty," Caroline returned, just barely managing to regain her composure.

Neither one of them ate much after that. Caroline toyed with the food on her plate, but her appetite had vanished, and with it her will to fight.

Standing, she carried her plate to the sink and scraped it clean. Paul brought over his dishes and they worked silently together, cleaning away the dinner mess.

"Paul," she said, after he'd wiped the last dish dry, "do you play Scrabble?" She knew he must; she'd seen the game on his shelf.

"A bit. Why?"

"Could you and I play? To help pass the evening?"

"I suppose."

For the first time in two days, Caroline's smile was natural and real. Her aunts loved Scrabble and had taught it to her as a child. With such expert tutoring, she was practically unbeatable. Her whole world became brighter. "It would be far more interesting, though," she said with a feigned thoughtful look, "if we played for something, don't you think?"

"How do you mean?"

She brought the game down from the shelf and unfolded the board. "Simple. If I win you'd grant me one request, and vice versa."

"And of course you'd ask for a divorce. No way."

"No, not a divorce." She'd work up to that.

"If not a divorce, what would you request?"

"Privacy."

"Privacy?"

"Yes, I want to sleep alone."

Skeptical, he eyed the recliner. "For how long?"

She'd go easy on him. "One night."

"Agreed." He pulled up a chair, twisted it around and straddled it. "And on the off chance I win?" He could see the mischief in her brilliant blue eyes. She clearly expected to beat him.

"Yes?" She regarded him expectantly. "What would you want?"

"A kiss."

"A kiss?"

"And not a peck on the cheek either. I want you to kiss me so well it'll turn me inside out." Not that it would take much, he mused.

Caroline hesitated. "But no more than a kiss, right?"

"No more. Agreed?"

With a saucy grin, she stuck out her hand. "Agreed." They shook on it and Caroline laughed. It felt so good to laugh again; she hated the constant bickering. Besides, this was going to be like taking candy from a baby.

"Let the games begin," Paul said, grinning back at her.

For a moment, it was hard to take her gaze off him. His eyes were smiling and although she couldn't see the rest of his face through the beard, she felt he must be a handsome man. His eyes certainly were appealing. Playfully, she held up her hand and flexed all her fingers.

"You draw first." In gentlemanly fashion, Paul handed her the small velvet bag with the letters of the alphabet.

Caroline inserted her hand and drew out an A. She gave him a triumphant look and set it on her letter holder. "I go first."

"Right."

It wasn't until they were a couple of plays into the game that Caroline recognized Paul's skill. He was going to provide some stiff competition. In fact, their scores remained close throughout the match. Caroline was down to her last five letters when Paul gained a triple word slot, added up his score and beamed her a proud look.

"Paul!" Caroline glanced at the board and gasped, unable to hold back her shock. "That's a four-letter word! A dirty four-letter word!"

"I'm well aware of that, love."

"You can't use that. It…it's indecent."

"It's also in the dictionary. Would you care to challenge me?"

She knew if she did, she'd immediately forfeit the game. "No," she grumbled. "But I consider that word in poor taste."

Paul's response was a soft chuckle. "You can challenge me if you wish."

"What's the score?" Five letters left... If she could use them all, she might be able to pull into the lead.

"Three hundred and twenty to two eighty-eight," Paul informed her gleefully. "Do you concede?"

"Never!"

"I'm afraid you have to. I'm out of letters."

"You won," Caroline said, almost in a daze. She'd lost only one game of Scrabble since her junior year in high school. She'd played brilliantly, yet Paul had outdone her.

"Yes, love, I won."

For a minute all she could do was stare at the board in shocked disbelief.

"Love? I believe you owe me a kiss."

She should object to his calling her "love," but she was too bemused. "You beat me at Scrabble," she said. "And I'm a good player. Very good."

"I'm fairly well versed in the game myself," Paul said. "There's not much else for Walter and me to do on those long winter nights."

Caroline's eyes narrowed. He'd known all along that he had an excellent chance of winning.

"I believe you owe me a kiss," he said again.

"You cheated," Caroline cried. "You used a four-letter word and—"

"Don't tell me you're a poor sport, too."

As fast as she could, Caroline removed the wooden pieces from the playing board. "You mean in addition to being a liar and a thief."

"I didn't say that," Paul told her soberly.

"Well, you needn't worry, I'll give you what I promised, but I still think it's unfair of you to use that word."

"You'd use it, too, if you had to," Paul said, folding up the game and placing it back on the bookcase.

"I wouldn't!"

"If you were down to four letters and that word placed you on a triple word score and would guarantee you a win, then I don't doubt you'd use it!"

"Well," Caroline hedged, a smile lifting the edges of her mouth. "I'd be tempted, but I don't think I'd stoop that low."

"Yes, you would. Now pay up, love."

Reluctantly, Caroline stood and rounded the table to his side.

"A kiss that'll turn me inside out," he reminded her.

"I remember," she said ruefully. She stood in front of him and Paul's arm circled her waist, pulling her onto his lap. She offered him a weak smile and set her hands on his shoulders. His palms slid around her back, directing her actions.

She twisted her head to the right, then changed her mind and moved it to the left. Slowly, she bent forward and placed her parted mouth on his. Paul's lips were moist and warm and brushed hers in a slow, sensuous way. Then his kiss grew wilder, and she responded with equal intensity.

They broke apart, panting and drained.

"Oh, Caroline," he breathed against her neck. Their mouths fused again. Although she'd initially had no intention of giving him more than the one kiss, she felt as eager for the second as he was.

Again his mouth nuzzled her neck. "Another game, Caroline, love? Only this time the stakes will be slightly higher."

Five

"Another game of Scrabble?" Caroline repeated, feeling content.

Dream or not, her memory served her well; Paul Trevor was one fantastic kisser. Suddenly her eyes flew open and she jerked herself free from Paul's arms. Mere hours before she'd vowed to freeze him out and here she was, sitting on his lap with her arms around his neck, kissing him with all the fervor in her heart.

"Our Scrabble days are over, Paul Trevor," she said coldly, placing her hand on the table to help maintain her balance. She felt a heated flush in her cheeks.

"You mean you're quitting because I'm a better player than you?" Paul returned with a laugh.

"Better player, my foot!"

The whole situation appeared to amuse him, which only angered Caroline more. She stormed into the bedroom and sat on the end of the bed, sulking. Until she'd met Paul, she'd considered herself an easygoing, fun-loving person. In two days' time he'd managed to change all that. With her arms crossed, she fumed, contemplating a hundred means of making him suffer.

It wasn't until they were in bed, Paul asleep at her side, that Caroline acknowledged the truth—she was more furious with herself than Paul. He'd played an honorable Scrabble game, except for that four-letter word, and had won their wager fair and square. What infuriated her most was her overwhelming response to his kiss. She didn't *want* to feel this way; it was far too difficult to hate him when he was so loving, so gentle, so…exciting.

In the morning, Paul woke her. "Time to get up, sleepyhead," he whispered in her ear.

Caroline's eyes fluttered open. Paul sat on the edge of the bed, smiling down at her. "Coffee's ready," he said.

"Paul," she pleaded, trying to appeal to his better nature. "Do I have to go to the pumping station with you again? It's so boring. I hate it."

"I'm sorry, love."

"I promise I won't pull any tricks."

He stood, shaking his head. "No, Caroline, you're coming with me."

Arguing would do no good, she realized with a frown, and tossed aside the heavy quilts to climb out of bed, grumbling as she did. Paul left her to dress in privacy, for which she was grateful.

Caroline prepared herself for the long, tedious hours. She took a deck of cards, some reading material and a pen and paper.

As he had the day before, Paul joined her at the desk beside hers a couple of hours into the morning. He smiled as he pulled out the ledger.

She waited to be sure she wasn't disturbing him before speaking. "Paul, who does the cooking for you?"

He didn't look up from the ledger as he spoke. "Tanana Eagleclaw. You met her the day you got here."

"There were so many people," she explained feebly.

He grinned, but didn't tease her about her memory lapse.

"Paul." She tried again. "I'm a good cook." That might have been a bit of an exaggeration, she added silently, but anything was better than sitting around this infernal pumping station ten hours a day.

"Hmm." He barely acknowledged her, apparently finding his ledgers more compelling.

"Really, I'm an excellent cook." She was getting desperate now. "I could prepare our meals. In fact, I'd like to do it."

"Tanana does an admirable job."

"Yes, but I want to do it!"

"You can't."

"Why not?"

"Because you're here with me, that's why not."

"Do you mean to tell me you're going to drag me here for the rest of my life?"

Paul sighed expressively. "We're going over the same territory as yesterday. You'll stay with me until I feel I can trust you again."

"Wonderful," she said in a sour voice. She couldn't begin to guess when that might be.

* * *

A week passed and each morning a sleepy Caroline traipsed behind Paul to the pumping station and each night she followed him home. No amount of pleading could get him to change his mind. He wanted her where he could see her every minute of every day. But, despite herself, she took comfort from his presence—even if she'd never admit as much.

The mail was delivered twice a week and a letter was sitting on the table addressed to Mr. and Mrs. Paul Trevor when they arrived back from the station during Caroline's second week in Gold River.

"A letter!" Caroline cried, as excited as a child on Christmas morning. Contact with the outside world. A tie with the past. She hurriedly read the return address. "It's from my aunts."

Paul smiled. "The two schemers?"

Eagerly, Caroline tore open the envelope. "The very ones." She hadn't forgiven them for their underhanded method of getting her to Alaska, but she missed them dreadfully.

"What do they have to say?" Paul coaxed.

"They're asking how I like my surprise. In case you don't know, that's you."

"And?" he prodded with a soft chuckle.

"And what?"

"How do you like me?"

It was Caroline's turn to laugh. "I find you...surprising."

"Typical."

"Aunt Mabel, she's the romantic one, says she feels that we're going to be happy and have...oh my goodness."

"What?"

Color seeped up from Caroline's neck and flushed her cheeks. "She predicts seven children, which is how many my great-great-grandmother had as a mail-order bride."

"I'm willing," Paul informed her with a grin.

"Be quiet, I'm reading. And Aunt Ethel…" She hesitated, her eyes scanning the rest of the page. "It was nothing." With her heart pounding frantically, and hoping to appear nonchalant, she refolded the letter and placed it back inside the envelope.

Paul joined her at the kitchen table. "What did she say?"

Caroline dropped her gaze. "It wasn't important."

"Shall I read the letter myself?"

"No…" she said and hid it behind her back. He could have insisted she hand it over, but didn't, although his cutting gaze reminded her that the letter had been addressed to both of them and he had every right to read it. "She told me that Larry Atkins dropped by when…

when he couldn't get hold of me. Aunt Ethel said she took great delight in telling him I'm a married woman now."

"I see," Paul said thoughtfully.

"I'm sure you don't." Caroline braced her hands against the kitchen counter as she fought a bout of self-pity. Her relationship with Larry had been over weeks before she'd come to Alaska. It shouldn't hurt this much now, but it did. Her heart yearned to know why he'd contacted her and how he'd reacted to the news that she was married to Paul. She wanted to inform Larry that it wasn't a real marriage —not the way theirs would have been.

Paul placed his hands on her shoulders. "Caroline, here." He turned her into his arms and held her quietly. It wasn't the embrace of a lover, but that of a caring, loyal friend.

She laid her face against his chest and drew in a wobbly breath. His hand was in her hair, stroking the back of her head in a soothing, comforting motion.

"Do you still love him?" he asked after a moment.

Caroline had to analyze her feelings. She'd been crazy in love with Larry for months. She missed him, thought about him often, wished him the best. But did she love him?

As she pondered his question, Paul decided that holding Caroline was the closest thing to heaven he'd ever experienced. He'd barely touched her in a week, wanting to give her time to know him. Their relationship was in an awkward stage; he wasn't convinced he could trust her yet. She'd outright told him that the first time he left her alone, she'd run away. Winter was coming on, and for her own safety he couldn't leave her until he was sure she wouldn't try to escape. He ached to hold her and kiss her until he felt he'd go mad. His successful restraint should make him a candidate for sainthood, he thought wryly. He regretted that he hadn't made love to her on their wedding night, and yet he'd never coerce Caroline or any woman, never force himself on her.

From her ramblings that night, Paul knew about Larry. The situation was less than ideal and he'd played the role of patient husband, difficult though that was. She'd been with him nine days, and yet it had aged him a hundred life-times to be with her—at meals, at the station, especially in bed—knowing her mind was on another man. A man who'd rejected her, for that matter.

"Caroline," he pressed, needing to know. "Do you still love him?"

"I...yes," she answered truthfully, her voice strained and low. This was diffi-cult. Paul was her husband, in fact if not in deed, and she couldn't deny either her attraction to him or his kindness to her.

She had no desire to be cruel to him. "You don't stop loving people because they've hurt you," she told him softly, relishing the comfort of his arms. "I'm trying not to love him…. Does that help?"

Tenderly, Paul kissed the side of her face. "It makes it easier to accept. I appreciate what it cost you to be honest."

A polite knock at the door drew them reluctantly apart. A very pregnant young woman walked in. Her smile was almost bashful, as though she felt she'd intruded on their lovemaking. "Did you need me, Paul?"

"Yes." Paul slipped his arm around Caroline's waist. "Caroline, this is Tanana Eagleclaw. Tanana, my wife, Caroline."

"How do you do, Mrs. Trevor?" the girl said formally.

"Fine, thank you, Tanana. And please call me Caroline. When is your baby due?" From the way she looked, it could've been any day.

"Six weeks." Again the young woman smiled shyly, obviously pleased about the pregnancy.

Caroline guessed she was in her early twenties. "You're a very good cook."

"Thank you."

Paul said something to her in her native tongue and Tanana nodded eagerly, her gaze moving briefly to Caroline. She left soon afterward.

"What was that all about?" Caroline asked.

"You said you wanted to meet Tanana, so I had her come over."

"But that wasn't the only reason. What did you say to her?"

"When?"

"Just now." Caroline gave him a bewildered look until she realized he was purposely playing dumb. "Never mind. You obviously don't want me to know, so forget it." She did understand one thing; Tanana's feelings would be hurt if Caroline were to take over the cooking. Perhaps when her baby was born, Caroline could assume the task without causing any loss of pride. If she was still here, of course...

That night, sitting in front of the fireplace, Caroline wrote her aunts a long reply. She told them that in the beginning she was furious with what they'd done, but gradually she'd changed her mind. Paul was a good man, a decent man, she wrote, and in that regard, she told the truth. But she couldn't tell them that she hoped and prayed that, given time, Paul would let her return to Seattle. That kind of information would only upset them, and there was no need to disillusion those two romantics. Nor did she say that if she was going to be a bride, she wanted the opportunity to choose her *own* husband. When Paul sent her back, and Caroline believed he would, there'd be time enough to explain everything. For now, she'd play their game and let them think they'd outsmarted her and that she was a happy, blushing bride. It could do no harm.

That night, Caroline fell into bed, exhausted. Paul joined her a little later, and as she did every night, she pretended to be asleep when he slipped in beside her.

"'Night, love," he whispered.

She didn't respond and a few minutes later drifted into a natural, contented sleep.

A noise woke her. She stirred—discovering that she'd been sleeping with her head on Paul's chest. His arm secured her to him.

"Is it morning yet?" she murmured,

closing her eyes again, reluctant to leave the warmth pressing against her.

"In a few minutes."

Paul rose before her every morning to stoke the fire and put on the coffee. Caroline had no idea whether she touched him in her sleep and feared that she'd wake in his arms one morning and embarrass them both.

"Do I do this often?" she asked, a little flustered.

"Not nearly enough," he returned. His hand ran down the length of her spine, stopping at the small of her back. He paused and inhaled sharply.

Caroline realized it was that soft rumble from his throat that had awakened her. Still she didn't move. He felt incredibly good—warm, strong…male.

Five minutes passed, then ten. Caroline knew she had to pull herself away; each minute was more pleasant than the one before.

"I'll make the coffee this morning," she murmured, easing away from him.

Paul stopped her. "There's no rush. Go back to sleep if you'd like."

"To sleep?" She lifted her head enough to search his face. "Aren't you going to the station?"

"I'll be there, but you won't."

Caroline was sure she'd misunderstood him.

"I asked Tanana to spend the day with you," he explained. "She's going to introduce you to the other women in the village."

For a moment, Caroline was too stunned to grasp what he was saying. "Paul, do you mean it? I don't have to go to the station?" Without thought, she wrapped her arms around his neck and covered his cheeks and forehead with a series of tiny, eager kisses.

Paul's hands found her head and guided her mouth to his for a kiss that was long and hard. Leisurely, her lips moved against his. Without her being certain how it happened, Paul reversed their positions with such ease that she lay on her back, staring up at him. Slowly, as though he couldn't resist her a second longer, he lowered his mouth to hers in a kiss that stirred her, heart and soul. Caroline couldn't possibly have denied herself that kiss. Her hands sought his face, luxuriating in the feel of his beard.

Paul broke off the kiss and, with a sigh that seemed to come from deep inside, buried his face in the hollow of her throat.

Caroline entwined her arms around his neck and released her own sigh of contentment. She was shocked at how right it felt to have Paul hold and kiss her. Her heart raged to a primitive beat and her body throbbed with a simmering passion. She didn't want to feel these things. When she left him, she didn't want to be weighed down with regrets.

He raised his head then, and compelled her gaze to meet his own, but she turned her head. "You're going to be late."

He nodded.

No time clock waited for him, and they both knew it. He eased away from her and sat on the edge of the bed for a moment to regain his strength. Caroline made him weak in ways he didn't understand. She wanted him; he could almost taste her eagerness. And yet, she had to say *yes* to him with complete certainty. With commitment as well as desire.

Exasperated, he plowed his fingers through his hair. He'd be patient a little longer, but he wasn't going to be able to withstand many more of her kisses. She fascinated him. She'd captured his heart and held it in the palm of her hand with as much concern as she would an unwanted sweet.

* * *

Although it was midmorning, Caroline was barely up and dressed when Tanana arrived. Again the young woman knocked politely at the door before stepping inside.

"Morning, Mrs. Trevor," she said shyly. "Caroline…"

"Morning, Tanana. I was just fixing myself some breakfast. Would you like some?"

She shook her head. "You come now, please?"

"Now?"

Tanana nodded.

"There isn't time for breakfast?"

"No time."

Muttering disparaging words under her breath, Caroline removed the skillet from the stove and put the eggs back in the refrigerator while Tanana grabbed Caroline's boots and parka.

"Where are we going?"

"The meeting hall."

"The other women are already there?"

"Yes. Many of them."

Caroline had no idea what they were waiting for, but she was so pleased to be able to talk to another human being that she wouldn't have cared if they were only going to sit around and drink weak coffee.

As Tanana had promised, there were seven or eight women gathered inside the large hall that served as the heart of the small community. Smiling faces greeted her when they walked in and Tanana led an astonished Caroline to an empty chair that stood in the center of the room—obviously the seat of honor.

She soon recognized that the women were giving a party in her honor, something like a bridal shower. One by one, each woman stepped forward and offered her a gift. Not all the women spoke English, but Tanana acted as their interpreter. The gifts were mostly homemade, displaying such talent and skill that Caroline's breath caught in her throat at their beauty. She received a stunning hand-knit sweater, slippers made from sealskin, several pieces of intricate scrimshaw with scenes that depicted Indian life in the frozen North, as well as smoked salmon and venison. Caroline watched in wide-eyed wonder as they approached her. When it came to material things, they had so little and she had so much, yet they were lovingly sharing a precious part of their lives. Tears gathered in her eyes and she swallowed down a thickness forming in her throat, not wanting to embarrass these friendly, generous women.

When they'd finished, Caroline stood and went to each one to personally thank her. Later, after they'd served lunch, the women gathered their yarn and started to knit.

"What are they making?" Caroline asked Tanana.

"Sweaters for the tourists."

"Gold River gets that many tourists?"

"Some, but they're mostly for the stores in Fairbanks, Juneau and Anchorage."

"Oh."

"All the women of the village work on the sweaters in wintertime," Tanana continued. "Each day we meet here."

"I knit, too," Caroline said, broaching the subject carefully. She wanted to be part of this community—at least, for as long as she lived here. Although her skill might not have been at the level of these women, she could learn. They'd been so kind to her that she wanted to return their kindness.

"Would you like to join us?" Tanana asked politely.

"Please." A moment later, Caroline was handed a pair of needles, several skeins of thick yarn and, with Tanana to guide her, was set to work.

That night, Caroline was bursting with excitement, so much that she could hardly contain it. When Paul walked in the cabin door, she practically flew across the room.

"Hi," she greeted him. "Did you know about the…party?"

His smiling eyes delved into hers. "Tanana told me about it last week. She said it was time I let you out of bed long enough to meet the village women."

Caroline decided to ignore that comment. "They're wonderful people."

"I know, love." Once he'd removed his parka and hung it in the closet, Caroline grabbed his hand and led him into the bedroom. She'd placed the nonfood items on the quilt for him to examine. He picked up each piece and nodded his pleasure at the village's generosity, praising the skill and beauty of their art. When he came to the oddly shaped piece of knitting, he regarded it skeptically. "And what's this?"

"Oh, yes, I nearly forgot. The women knit, but I guess you already know that. Anyway, they let me sit and work with them this afternoon. Of course I'm not nearly as good as they are and my poor sweater wouldn't be anywhere near good enough to sell to the tourists." She laughed. "It's funny to think that some tourist might buy a sweater assuming it was knit by a local Athabascan only to discover it was made by a Seattle nurse." She giggled again. "At the end of the afternoon, I think Tanana was afraid of hurting my feelings so I asked if I could do something else with my first effort."

"And what was that?"

"I told them I wanted to knit this sweater for you."

"What did they say to that?"

"Oh, they were pleased, but then they would be, since they probably couldn't sell it." She waltzed out of the bedroom and into the kitchen. "And I made dinner. Tanana looked so tired that I offered. Naturally, she argued with me, but not too strenuously."

"So you had a good day."

"I had a marvelous day!" She turned her back to him to stir the simmering gravy. All afternoon she'd been trying to come up with a way of persuading Paul that she should join the other women on a daily basis. He'd been so unyielding in other matters that she dreaded a confrontation now.

"I suppose you want to go back?"

Caroline whirled around, her heart in her eyes. "Yes. Are you okay with that?"

"I think it's more your decision than mine."

She understood what he was saying,

but bit back a ready reply while she took slices of meat from the oven and forked them onto a platter, which she set on the table.

"Unless you trust me again," she said, her eyes holding his, "I know I won't ever be able to prove I'm trustworthy in your eyes."

"Then do as you wish."

Caroline was so pleased that she was hard-pressed not to throw her arms around his neck and kiss him the way she had that morning. It wasn't until after they'd eaten that she realized how much she actually wanted to kiss him, but quickly pushed the thought from her mind.

Later, she found herself humming while washing the dinner dishes, and paused, surprised at herself. She was happy—truly content. She turned to find Paul watching her as he dried their plates and they shared a smile.

Once again they played a heated game of Scrabble, but without any wagers. This time Caroline won.

"You'll note that I didn't use a single dirty word," she told him with a proud snicker.

Paul chuckled and reset the board for a second game.

That next afternoon and for several more that followed, Caroline joined the village women for their daily knitting session. The first few days, the women were shy and didn't say much to her. Gradually they opened up and she became privy to the village gossip. More than one of the women seemed to find something about Caroline amusing. Every time they looked in her direction, they leaned over to the woman next to them and whispered something that made the other smile. Finally, when

Caroline's curiosity got the better of her, she asked Tanana about it.

The young woman blushed. "They say you are a fortunate woman."

"Fortunate? I don't understand."

"Yes, you have Paul for your lover. They are envious that at night he sleeps at your side and holds you in his arms. They say you will have many healthy babies with Paul. He is…I don't know the English word."

"Never mind," Caroline returned, her fingers tightening around the knitting needles. "I know what you mean." Did she ever! So Paul was a virile male who had sampled the delights of the village women before her arrival.

By the time she got back to the cabin, Caroline was so furious that she paced the small enclosure, ready to give her husband a piece of her mind the instant he returned home. She'd never dreamed, hadn't thought he'd ever do anything that low. No wonder he wanted a wife. From the looks the women had been sending her way, they'd probably started fighting over him. Well, they could have him. She was finished with him. Nothing could keep her in Gold River now. She didn't care what it took, she was leaving Paul just as soon as she could.

When the wooden door opened and the howling wind whirled through the cabin, it was only a spring breeze compared to the ice around Caroline's heart.

"Hi," Paul said with a grin, but one look at her contorted, angry features and his smile quickly faded. "What's wrong?"

She didn't wait for him to remove his coat. Her index finger found its mark in the middle of his chest. "You are despicable. You are lower than a snake. You are..." Words failed her as hot tears blurred her vision. "I can't find the words to tell you how much I despise you!"

Paul didn't look particularly concerned. "Was it something I said, or are you still mad about that four-letter word I used in the Scrabble game?"

Six

"You think you're so clever, don't you?" Caroline flared. Her outrage got the better of her and she picked up a book from the end table and hurled it at him.

With a dexterity few could manage, Paul caught the book and the saltshaker that immediately followed. The amusement fled his eyes. "Caroline, what's gotten into you?"

"You…animal!"

"Tell me what I did."

"You...*beast!*" The pepper shaker whizzed past his ear.

"Caroline!"

"You...you...adulterer!" That might not make complete sense, since he hadn't been married, but it conveyed her disgust.

Stunned, Paul watched as she stormed into the bedroom and viciously slammed the door. For a minute he did nothing but stand with a book and salt-shaker in his hand, too bemused to move. Beyond her explosive fury, what shocked Paul most was the hurt he saw in her eyes.

"Adulterer?" he repeated in an astonished whisper.

Inside the room, Caroline sat on the edge of the bed. Stinging tears threatened to run down her face and she rubbed the heels of her hands against her eyes in a futile effort to restrain them. Damn it all, she was falling in love with him—head over heels in love with a man who had neither morals nor conscience. If she didn't love him, then knowing what he'd done wouldn't hurt this much. Caroline cried harder. She didn't *want* to love him. A hiccupping sob ripped through her throat and she buried her face in her hands.

Her crying devastated Paul. He'd planned to wait until her anger had dissipated before trying to reason with her, but he couldn't. Every sob felt like a punch to his abdomen.

"Caroline," he called from the other side of the door. "Can we talk about this?"

Silence.

"Caroline, believe me, I haven't the foggiest idea what you're talking about."

"I'll just bet you don't!"

"I don't." He tried the knob, but she'd locked the door. "As your husband, I demand that you open this door immediately." He felt foolish saying it, but couldn't think of anything else.

She snickered.

"Caroline... Please." When she didn't respond, he rammed his hands in his pants pockets. "Are you angry about our wedding night? Is that it?" Standing directly in front of the door, he muttered, "I can see it isn't going to do any good to try talking to you now. You're in no mood to be reasonable."

With that, the bedroom door opened so unexpectedly that he almost fell through.

Caroline glared at him with renewed animosity. "Do you mean to tell me that...that on the night we were married you...you took advantage of me?"

"Caroline, if you'd listen..."

"O-o-h." Her clenched fists pummeled his chest until her hands felt numb with pain.

"That's enough." Paul caught her

wrists and pinned her against the wall. Her shoulders heaved with exertion, and tears streaked her face and brimmed in her wide, blue eyes.

Trembling, she collected herself and drew in a ragged breath. Briefly, she struggled, but Paul's hold tightened. His fierce look held her as effectively as his hands. Caroline met his eyes with open defiance.

"Love." His voice was a hoarse whisper of bewilderment and confusion, his face mere inches from her own. "What is it?"

He spoke with such gentleness that it would be easy to forget what he was and what he'd done. "Let me go," she said, her rage gone now, replaced by a far deeper, more crippling emotion—sorrow.

Paul saw the pain in her eyes and was filled with such perplexity that he reacted instinctively. In an effort to comfort, his mouth sought hers.

His kiss was insistent, demanding, relentless. Almost against her will Caroline parted her lips to meet his. Her eagerness for him grew, an eagerness that rocked her soul. Gradually both she and Paul relaxed, the crucial need abated. He loosened his grip, but continued to hold her wrists. Caroline became aware of the heavy thud of his heart while her own pulsed with a frantic rhythm.

They breathed in unison. Paul's eyes searched her face as he looked for any clue that would help him understand her irrational behavior. Hot color stained her cheeks, but he didn't know if it was from her anger or her excitement during their kiss. Her lips were moist, and he bent his head to taste their sweetness again. When he finally drew back, he and Caroline were both trembling.

He released her hands and Caroline dropped them to her sides. "I was with the women today," she began, in a voice so fraught with pain that Paul wrapped her securely in his arms. "And they told me..."

"Told you what, Caroline?"

"That...you're a fantastic lover."

He frowned. "Ah," he whispered slowly, then cupped her face with his hands, kissing her briefly. "And you assumed they meant it literally?"

"How else was I supposed to take it?"

"I've been living here for several years now," he began. "I've become friends with many of them and their families. They're, uh, kind enough to favor me with certain attributes they *believe* I possess."

Caroline's gaze met his. "They sounded so...so knowledgeable."

He grinned widely. "Hey, I'm only

one man. I couldn't possibly have had that many lovers."

"Have you had…even one?" Her intense gaze locked with his.

"By everything I hold dear, I swear to you that I've never had a single lover in Gold River." Paul had assumed she'd welcome his assurance, but his words produced the most uncanny response; tears flooded her eyes and streamed down her face. Caroline hugged him fiercely, burying her face in his sweater. Half laughing, half crying, she lifted her head and spread eager kisses mingled with salty tears on his face. Gently Paul held her, wondering if he'd been outside civilization so long he'd lost his ability to understand women. He sighed; perhaps he had.

Their relationship altered after that night. The changes were subtle ones and came about so naturally that Paul could only guess their meaning. The first thing he noticed was that Caroline had placed her suitcase under the bed, as though she'd finally accepted her position in his life and planned to remain. He yearned for her to forget her hope of returning to Seattle.

He knew she spent a lot of time with Tanana and apparently they'd worked out an agreement concerning dinner, since Caroline started cooking all their meals. She'd once told him she was an excellent cook and he learned that she hadn't exaggerated. She was clever, inventive and resourceful. It wasn't every woman who could make dried eggs edible.

Everyone was her friend; even Walter had become her ally. Paul had been in the village six months before the old man had fully accepted him. Walter's acceptance of Caroline was typical of the love she received from all the peo-

ple of Gold River. The children adored
her; Caroline couldn't walk out the door
without two or three of them running
to her side. One day Paul discovered
Caroline in the meeting hall, skipping
rope with the sixth-grade girls. Another
day he found her involved in a heated
soccer game with the junior-high boys.

When an old woman had a toothache,
she came to Caroline. A feverish baby
was brought to her as well. A little boy
with a stomach ache showed up unexpectedly one afternoon. The medical
clinic was open once a week when a
team from the Public Health Department flew in for appointments, but it
was Caroline the villagers came to. At
first she used her own personal quantity
of painkillers and bandages; then, as a
qualified nurse she received access to
the clinic's supply. Paul felt absolutely
delighted that she could use her training this way.

But now he was so much in love he thought he'd die from wanting her. But to rush into lovemaking now would be foolish. She was so close to recognizing she loved him, and when that day came it would be right and beautiful, although he often wondered how much longer he could hold out. He endured the sweetest torture every morning when he woke to find her in his arms. At night, the agony was far greater; he dreaded her touch and at the same time craved it.

That evening after dinner, Caroline brought out a large package and placed it on the ottoman in front of him.

Paul lowered the two-day-old newspaper and raised questioning eyes to his wife. "What's this?"

"Open it and see." She'd worked so hard on this sweater that if it didn't fit, she'd burst into tears. "I probably should've saved it for Christmas, but..." It was silly to be this nervous.

She wanted to please him and the holidays were still six weeks away. Besides, she couldn't think of a better way to tell Paul she loved him.

"But what, love?"

"But I thought you deserved it now." For calming her angry tirades, for being so patient with her, for his gentleness and a hundred other admirable qualities. And because she longed to be his wife in the truest sense of the word.

Carefully, Paul removed the paper and held up the Irish cable-knit sweater. "Caroline, I'm...stunned. It's a fine piece of work."

"If it doesn't fit, I can redo it." She couldn't believe she'd made that offer; the pattern was difficult and complicated. If it hadn't been for Tanana's and the other women's help, she would've given up and unraveled the sweater weeks before.

"I'm sure it'll fit perfectly." To prove

his point, he stood and pulled it over his head. "Where did you get the yarn?" he asked, running his hand over the sleeves. The sweater was a lovely shade of winter wheat and far lighter than the material the village women typically used.

"I sent away for it. Mary Finefeather had a catalog."

"How did you pay for it?" She'd never come to him for money, although he would've been more than pleased to give it to her. They had little need for cash in Gold River. The supply store and grocery sent him monthly accounts and his paychecks were automatically deposited in the Fairbanks Savings and Loan.

"I used my credit card."

He nodded and kissed her lightly. "Thank you, love. I'll always treasure it."

Caroline's returning smile was weak,

as though she was disappointed by his response. Paul watched her leave and wondered if he'd said something to offend her. He began to doubt that he'd ever understand her.

Hours later, Paul lay at her side. His even breathing convinced Caroline he was sound asleep as she lay on her back wide-eyed, staring at the ceiling. She was now convinced that she was a failure. For two weeks, she'd been trying to tell Paul that she was ready to be his wife in *every* way. How a man could be so completely blind was beyond her. If it hadn't been for a few secret looks of longing she'd intercepted, she would have abandoned her cause. She made excuses to be close to him, to touch him. All the signals she'd been sending him would have stopped a freight train! The sweater had been her ace in the hole and even that had failed. In return, he'd kissed her like an affectionate older brother.

Ah well, there was always tomorrow. Maybe if she wore the nightgown her aunts had given her... She smiled and her eyes drifted shut. She couldn't get any more obvious than that.

The next day was a busy one. The small town was holding an early Thanksgiving feast, and it seemed half of Alaska had been invited. People had been arriving from the outlying areas all morning. Caroline and Tanana were responsible for decorating the meeting hall and the two of them made a comical sight. Caroline wouldn't allow Tanana, who was in an advanced stage of pregnancy, to climb the ladder to hang the crepe-paper streamers, so Caroline wrapped them around her neck and hauled them up herself.

"This isn't fair," Tanana complained. "All I'm doing is holding the ladder for you."

"I'm not going to let you stand on this rickety old thing," Caroline muttered, stretching as far as her limbs would allow to stick a thumbtack into the beam.

"If Paul ever saw this, he'd be mad."

"He isn't going to know, and you're not going to tell him—right?"

"What will you bribe me with?"

Caroline laughed. "Hush, now, and hand me another streamer." She climbed down a couple of steps and Tanana gave her the next set of bright orange and yellow crepe-paper strips.

When they'd finished, the two women surveyed the hall, proud of their accomplishment. It was astonishing how much a little color added to the festive spirit.

Mary Finefeather, a foster grandmother to many of the village kids, delivered sandwiches to Caroline and Tanana. Typical of the old woman's personality, Mary spoke in choppy one-word sentences.

"Eat," she said with a grin.

"I think that's an order," Caroline commented, and looked at Tanana, who smiled in reply. The younger woman had lost much of her shyness now and Caroline considered her a valued friend.

"What are you getting Paul for Christmas?" Tanana asked, studying Caroline.

"I...don't know. I gave him the sweater last night." She wished she hadn't; with the holidays fast approaching, she had wasted her best gift—seemingly for naught.

"I know what he wants."

"You do?"

Tanana placed her hand on her swollen abdomen and stared at her stomach. "He wants a son."

Caroline nearly swallowed her sandwich whole. "Oh?"

"You'll give him fine sons? And daughters?"

Embarrassed, Caroline looked away. "Someday."

"Soon?"

"I...I don't know." Caroline couldn't very well announce that she and Paul had never made love, at least not that she could remember.

Caroline worked for part of the afternoon, then returned to the cabin, frustrated and tired. She'd slept poorly, and tonight would be another late night. Before she could talk herself out of the idea, she climbed onto the bed and closed her eyes, intending to rest for only a few minutes.

Paul found her there an hour later, barely visible in the soft light of dusk. He paused in the doorway of their bedroom and experienced such a wave of desire that he sucked in a tight breath. Her blouse had ridden up to expose the creamy smooth skin of her midriff. Blood pounded in his head and his feet seemed to move of their own accord, taking him to her side.

His gaze lingered on the smooth slant of her brow and a smile briefly touched his face. She could make a clearer statement with an arch of her eyebrow than some women said in twenty years. Her nose was perfect and her sweet, firm lips were enough to drive a man insane. He thought about the last time they'd kissed and how, for hours afterward, he'd been in a foul mood, barking at Walter and the others until Walter had suggested that Paul do something to cure whatever was ailing him.

Caroline was ailing him. He wanted to touch her, to—

Caroline yawned and rolled over.

Paul jumped away from her as though he'd been caught doing something wrong. His knees felt like slush in a spring thaw. On unsteady feet, he walked over to the dresser.

"Caroline, it's time to get up." He hardly recognized the strained, harsh voice as his own.

Slowly she opened her eyes. She'd been having the most wonderful dream about giving Paul the child Tanana claimed he wanted so badly. One look at her husband, who stood stiffly on the other side of the room, was enough to return her to the cold world of reality. His back was to her.

"Hi," she said, stretching her hands high above her head and yawning loudly.

"Hi," he said gruffly. He didn't dare turn around. If her midriff had been showing before, he could only imagine what he'd glimpse now. He felt himself go weak all over again.

Caroline frowned at his abruptness. "Did you have a good day?"

"Sure." He pulled open the top drawer and took out a clean T-shirt. "You'd better get dressed or we'll be late for the party."

"What time is it?"

"Five."

Caroline's frown deepened. No one was expected before seven. "We've got plenty of time."

No, we don't, Paul wanted to shout. He, for one, was at the end of his rope.

"Paul, what's wrong?"

"Nothing." He slammed the drawer shut with unnecessary force. "I just happen to think it's time you got out of bed."

"Are you angry because I took a nap?"

"No," he snapped.

She rose to a sitting position and released a long sigh. "Sometimes I don't understand you."

"That makes two of us."

"Will you please turn around? I don't like talking to your back." She made the request softly, confused by his mood. She'd never known Paul to be so short-tempered and illogical.

"If you don't mind, I'm busy."

Caroline blinked. She replayed the conversation with Tanana, and a heaviness settled on her shoulders. She loved Paul and yearned to have his child, but instead of growing together they seemed to be drifting apart. Sudden tears misted her eyes. She'd thought that once she acknowledged she was in love with him everything would be perfect. Instead, it had gotten worse—much worse.

Paul tossed his sweater on the bed. "Good grief, don't tell me you're crying! One day you're hurling saltshakers at me and the next you're weeping because I tell you to hurry and get ready for a party you've been working on all day."

Her eyes widened with determination to hold back the tears. "I'm not crying. That's ridiculous. Why should I be crying?"

He threw up his hands. "Who knows? I've given up trying to understand you."

The party was a grand success. The meeting hall was filled to the rafters with friends and loved ones from nearby communities. The dinner proved to be delicious and Caroline received rave reviews for her apple pies and decorating efforts. Although she smiled and made all the appropriate responses, she couldn't seem to get into the party mood.

When the tables were cleared and the dancing began, Caroline saw how Paul seemed to dance with every woman in the room but her. Not that Caroline was given much time to notice. One partner after another claimed her hand for a turn around the floor. After an hour, she pleaded exhaustion and sat down, fanning her flushed face with one hand.

To her surprise, Paul joined her, sitting in the chair beside hers. His lips were pinched, his face grim. "I imagine you're pleased to have every man for a hundred miles panting after you."

Caroline's mouth fell open at the unjust accusation. Quickly she composed herself, stiffening her back. "I'm going to forgive you for that remark, Paul Trevor, because you owe me one. But from here on we're even." She stood up and purposely walked away from him. Her eyes clouded by confusion, she nearly stumbled into Walter, and glancing up at him, hurriedly stammered an apology.

"Didn't you promise me this dance?" Walter said.

Still unable to find her tongue, Caroline nodded.

Studying her, the older man guided her onto the dance floor. A waltz was playing and Caroline slipped one arm around his neck and placed her hand in his.

"All right, girl, tell me—what's made you so unhappy?"

Caroline's mouth formed a poor excuse for a smile. "Paul. I don't know how any man can be so stupid."

"He's blinded by his love for you."

"I sincerely doubt that's it." Caroline looked directly into Walter's face. "I have the feeling he's ready to ship me back to Seattle." There'd been a time when she'd prayed for exactly that, but now her heart ached at the mere thought of leaving him.

Standing by the punch bowl, Paul watched her. Caroline could feel his dark gaze on her back. With every passing minute, his eyes grew darker and more angry.

Walter chuckled. "Paul would rather cut off his arm than send you away. Have you told him you love him?"

Caroline's shocked gaze clashed with the man's wise old eyes. "No."

"Then do it, and soon, before he makes an even bigger fool of himself."

When the dance ended, Walter delivered her to Paul's side and quietly left them. Caroline and Paul stood glaring at each other until the music started.

"Shall we?" Caroline asked, glancing toward the crowded floor.

"Why not? You've seen fit to dance with every other male here tonight."

"Paul," she whispered. "Are you jealous?"

He didn't answer her, but she saw that his face was as grim as she'd ever seen it. His hold on her was loose, as if he couldn't bear to touch her.

Caroline swallowed her pride. "There isn't anyone here I'd rather dance with than you."

Still he said nothing. His eyes were focused straight ahead and she didn't see so much as a flicker in his rock-hard features to indicate that he'd heard her or that her words had any effect.

"When I first came to Gold River, I hated it."

If possible, his mouth grew harder, more inflexible.

"But…things changed and I realized I was happy here. There's a wildness to this land. A challenge that makes people strong and wise. I've seen that in you and admired your patience and gentleness."

Momentarily, Paul dropped his eyes and studied her as though he didn't quite trust what she was saying.

Caroline thought her heart would

burst with pain when he quickly glanced away.

"You idiot," she said and brought her shoe down hard on the top of his foot.

Paul let out a small yelp of pain.

"I'm trying to tell you I love you, but you can forget it! And while you're at it, you can forget about our son, too!" She broke away and left him holding one leg like a flamingo while he nursed his injured foot.

At the door, Caroline grabbed her boots and parka and stormed out of the meeting hall, too angry for tears, too frustrated to consider what she was doing. She knew only that she had to escape.

"Caroline!"

His frantic call came to her before she reached the cabin door. With heightened resolve, she pretended she hadn't heard him.

"Caroline! Would you wait?"

She ignored his pleading as well. By the time he arrived, she was sitting by the fireplace with a book in front of her face.

"Caroline...what did you just say?" He was breathless, his voice rushed and uneven.

"It was nothing."

"It was everything," he whispered in awe. "*Do* you love me? Caroline, would you please look at me?"

"No."

Paul felt he was going to explode with happiness. "And what was that crazy remark about a son?"

She turned the page of her book and glanced with keen interest at the beginning of the next chapter, although she had no idea what was going on in the story.

Paul fell to his knees at her side and pried the book from her stiff fingers. She refused to meet his eyes.

"Caroline..." He breathed her name

with a heart overflowing with expectancy and hope. "Are you telling me you're ready to be my wife?"

"I couldn't have made it any plainer. I've flaunted myself in front of you all week. I gave you the sweater...hoping... Paul Trevor, you're an idiot! For days, I've been throwing myself at you and you...you've been so blind and so stupid."

"You have?" Paul was flabbergasted. "When? Days?"

"Weeks!"

"Weeks?" He *had* been blind, but no longer.

His hands framed her face as he guided her lips to his, kissing her with such hungry intensity it robbed her of breath. Somehow he lifted her from the chair, cradled her in his arms and carried her into their bedroom. He placed her on the mattress and knelt over her, studying her to be sure this wasn't a dream.

Caroline stared into his eyes and twined her arms around his neck, bringing his mouth back to her own. "You idiot," she whispered again.

"Not anymore, love."

Their lips met over and over, as though each kiss was sweeter and more potent than the one before. Holding back nothing, Caroline surrendered to him with joyful abandon. He explored her face, her neck, her shoulders, charting undiscovered territory with his lips as he helped her undress. Finally they were both free of restricting clothes and Paul kissed her until she responded with a wantonness she didn't know she possessed. They broke apart, winded and panting.

"Caroline," he murmured, his face keen and ardent in the moonlight. "Are you sure?"

"I've never been more sure of anything in my life."

* * *

Deeply content, Caroline lay with her cheek against her husband's chest. Her leg stroked his and she sighed her happiness. There was no turning back for them now; they were truly husband and wife, their commitment to each other complete.

Paul's hand smoothed the tumbled hair from her face. "Are you happy, love?"

"Very." Her nails scraped playfully at his chest. "Why didn't you tell me it was this good? If I'd known, I would've demanded my wifely rights." She raised her head to kiss the strong, proud line of his chin. "Tanana and the other women guessed correctly—you *are* a fantastic lover."

Paul opened his mouth to answer her when there was a loud knock on the front door. Caroline gave him a look of dismay; no one would come unless there was trouble.

Paul rolled to his feet, his body alert. He reached for his clothes and threw them on, then hurried to the door.

Caroline dressed in a rush, anxious now. When she entered the living room, she found Paul speaking to Thomas Eagleclaw, Tanana's husband.

"Tanana's gone into labor," Paul explained. "Her mother's with her, but she wants you."

Caroline nodded. "I'll be there in a minute."

Seven

By the time Caroline arrived at Tanana's cabin, her heart was pounding, not with exertion from the long walk, but with excitement and, she admitted, anxiety. Her experience was limited to a sterile hospital delivery room with a doctor, other nurses and all the necessary emergency equipment. None of that existed in Gold River, and Caroline had never felt more inadequate.

Thomas, Tanana's husband, and Paul led the way to their cabin. Tanana lay in the center of a double bed, her face glistening with perspiration, her eyes wide with pain. The young woman held out her hand to Caroline. "Thank you for coming."

"When did the contractions start?" Caroline asked, sitting on the edge of the bed.

Tanana lowered her gaze. "This afternoon."

"Why didn't you tell me?"

"I wasn't sure they meant I was in labor."

Caroline understood. Tanana had mentioned twice that week that she'd been experiencing "twinges" and Caroline had told her those were normal and she needn't worry.

The older woman in the bedroom rose to greet her. Tanana's mother smiled her welcome and returned to her rocking chair, content to let Caroline assume the role of midwife. Caroline went to the kitchen to wash her hands, praying silently that this would be an easy birth, routine in every way.

It wasn't. Hours later, both Caroline and Tanana were drenched in sweat. The girl was terrified. Caroline, although outwardly calm, was equally frightened. Tanana's mother continued to rock, offering an encouraging smile now and then.

"It shouldn't be long now," Caroline said, smoothing the hair from Tanana's brow and wiping her face with a cool washcloth.

Tanana tried to smile, but the effort was too great. "Rest as much as you can between pains," Caroline instructed.

Tanana nodded. She closed her eyes and rolled her head to the side, ruthlessly biting the corner of her lip as another contraction took hold of her body.

"Don't fight it," Caroline said. "Try to breathe through the pain."

Tanana's death grip on Caroline's fingers slackened and Caroline relaxed, too. "You're doing great, Tanana. I'll check you with the next contraction and we'll see how far things have progressed."

Caroline's worst fears were confirmed; the baby was breech. A knot of fear clogged her throat. Didn't this baby realize she didn't have a lot of experience in this area? The least it could do was cooperate! "I'm going to get some fresh water," she told Tanana, and stood to leave the bedside. Tanana's eyes revealed her fear. "Don't worry," Caroline said with a reassuring smile, "I'll be right back."

In the next room, Paul was playing cards with Thomas, although it was easy to see that neither man's attention was on the game. One look at Caroline's distraught eyes, and Paul moved to her side at the kitchen sink. "What's wrong?"

"The baby is breech. Paul, I'm frightened. This is far more complicated than anything I've ever handled. My training was all in a hospital setting, and I've worked in a doctor's office for two years. You don't get much experience delivering breech babies in an office building."

"Tanana needs you."

"I know." Paul was referring to strength and confidence, but she couldn't offer the poor girl something she didn't have herself.

"If you think it's more than you can cope with, we'll call in a plane and fly her to Fairbanks."

"Yes. Please call." But that would take hours and they both knew it. "In the meantime I'll...do my best."

"I know you will, love." His hands cradled her face and he kissed her, his lips fitting tenderly over hers, lending her his own strength. A whimper from

Tanana broke them apart and Caroline hurried back to her friend's side.

The hours sped by, but Caroline was barely aware of their passing. She was busy every minute, talking softly, encouraging Tanana, calling on not only her experience but her instincts. Her friend's fortitude and inner strength impressed her. When the squalling infant was finally released from the young woman's body, unrestrained tears of happiness filled Caroline's eyes.

"You have a son," she said, gently placing the baby on his mother's stomach.

"A son." Tanana's wide smile revealed her overwhelming delight and with a cry of joy, she fell back against the pillow.

A few minutes later, Caroline entered the kitchen, carrying the crying infant in her arms. Her eyes met Paul's as the two men rose slowly to their feet.

"A boy," she said softly.

Thomas let out a hoot of exhilarated happiness and paused to briefly inspect his son before he rushed past Caroline to join his wife.

Paul looked down at the small bundle in her arms. His eyes softened at the wrinkled face and tiny fingers protruding from the blanket. "You must be exhausted," he said, studying Caroline.

Lightly, she shook her head. She'd never experienced such a feeling of bliss in her life. It was as though she'd labored to deliver this child herself and he'd been born of her own body. "He's so beautiful." Unabashed tears rained from her eyes and she kissed the baby's sweet brow.

"Yes, but not as beautiful as you, love," Paul said tenderly, his heart constricting at the sight of a baby in his wife's arms. The day would come when they'd have a child of their own and the thought filled him with happy anticipation.

An hour later, the emergency medical team had been and gone, pronouncing both mother and son in good health. Paul took Caroline back to their cabin. Now that the surge of high spirits had faded, Caroline realized how weary she was. "What time is it?"

"Noon."

"*Noon?* Really?"

Paul led her directly into their bedroom and sat her on the bed, where she fell back on the rumpled sheets and heaved a sigh, closing her eyes. Smiling down at her, Paul removed her shoes.

"Paul?"

"Hmm?" He unzipped her jeans next and slid them down her long legs. A surge of desire shot through him and he forced himself to look at her face and remember how exhausted she was. Given the least amount of encouragement, he would've fallen into bed beside her.

"Tanana told me you wanted a son." Her eyes still closed, she felt lethargic, yet oddly contented.

"A daughter would do as well."

"Soon?"

"Sooner than you think if you don't get under these blankets," he grumbled, covering her with the quilts.

Caroline smiled, feeling warm and secure. "I love you," she murmured dreamily.

Paul stood by the edge of the bed, unsteady. "You love me?" She didn't answer him and he knew she was already asleep. His heart swelled with such joy that he felt like shouting and dancing around the small room. Instead, he bent down and kissed her temple. To stay with her now would be torture and although it was a different kind of agony, Paul left the room and curled up on the recliner, meaning only to rest his eyes.

Caroline found him there several hours later. "Paul," she whispered, shaking his shoulder.

With reluctance, he opened his eyes. When he saw it was Caroline, he grinned tiredly. "Did you sleep?"

"Like a baby. Why are you out here?"

"Because you needed your rest, love." His arm circled her waist and he brought her into his lap, where he nuzzled her neck. She felt so good in his arms, soft, feminine, his—all his. Larry was in the past now and gone forever.

Paul thought of his life before she'd come to him and wondered how he'd managed all those years without her. She was as much a part of him as his own heart. She was his world, his sun, his stars. All these weeks she'd led him down a rock-strewn trail, but every minute had been worth the wait. She was more than he'd ever dreamed.

Caroline smiled. Her hands directed his mouth to hers and she kissed him hungrily. He didn't need to tell her why he'd slept on the recliner; she knew and she loved him for it.

"Oh, Caroline," he groaned. "Do you realize what you're doing?"

She answered him by unfastening the buttons of his shirt and slipping her fingers inside to stroke his chest. The wild sensations he aroused in her were so exquisite, she wanted to weep.

The sounds of their lovemaking filled the cabin. Whispered phrases of awe followed as Paul removed her blouse.

"Caroline," he moaned. "If we don't stop right now, we're going to end up making love in this chair."

"I don't want to stop...."

In the days afterward, Caroline could hardly believe that they'd waited so long to become lovers when everything was so extraordinarily right between them. Now they seemed to be making up for lost time. His desire for her both delighted and astonished her. They made love every night and often Paul couldn't seem to wait until their usual bedtime. One evening, in the middle of a Scrabble game, she found him looking at her with a wild gleam in his eye.

"Paul?"

He glanced toward the bedroom and raised his brows in question.

"It's only seven o'clock," she said, laughing.

His expression was almost boyish. "I can wait…I think."

Caroline smiled, stood and walked around the table to take him by the hand. "Well, I can't."

They never finished playing Scrabble that night. Instead they invented new games.

Some days, Paul was barely in the door when he wanted her.

"What's for dinner?" he'd ask.

She'd tell him and catch that look in his eye and automatically turn down the stove. "Don't worry, it can simmer for an hour."

Their dinner simmered and they sizzled. This was the honeymoon they'd never had and Caroline prayed it would last a lifetime.

She yearned to get pregnant, but the first week of December, she discovered sadly that she wasn't.

"If the truth be known," Paul said comfortingly, "I'd rather have you to myself for a while."

Caroline nestled close to his side, her head in the crook of his arm. "It may not be so easy for me. My mother had difficulty getting pregnant."

"Then we'll just have to work at it, love."

Caroline laughed; if they worked any harder, they'd drop from sheer exhaustion. Paul kissed her and held her close.

"I never thought I'd find such happiness," he told her.

"Me neither." He wasn't a man of many words or flowery speeches. Nor did he shower her with expensive gifts. But his actions were far more effective than mere words. He loved her, and every day he did something to let her know how much he cared.

One morning after Paul had gone to work, Caroline realized she'd nearly let all this happiness slip through her fingers. The pain of Larry's rejection had nearly blinded her to Paul's love—and her own feelings. When Larry had left, Caroline had almost died inside. Now she realized how mismatched they were. They'd been friends, and had erroneously assumed their friendship meant they'd also be good lovers. Not until she'd slept with Paul could Caroline acknowledge that marriage to Larry would have been a mistake.

Larry had recognized the truth long before she did.

Undoubtedly, he was torturing himself with guilt. Her aunts had mentioned his visit in their first letter and although his name was brought up briefly in subsequent letters, Caroline knew he'd been back to visit her aunts, eager for word of her.

In an effort to ease her friend's mind, Caroline decided to write him a letter. It was the least she could do. He'd feel better and she could tell him herself how happy she was. She wished him the best and was eternally grateful that he'd had the wisdom and courage to keep them both from making a colossal mistake.

Caroline had originally intended her letter to be short, but by the time she was done, she'd written five pages. She told him about Paul and how much she loved her husband and thanked Larry for being her friend. She added bits and pieces about her life in Alaska and how beautiful the land was. Come summer, Paul had promised to take her hiking and fishing, and she joked with Larry because he got queasy at the sight of a worm. When she'd finished, Caroline read the letter and realized her happiness shone through every word. Larry would have no more doubts.

After stuffing the five pages into an envelope, Caroline carried the letter to the supply store, which also served as the local post office.

"Good afternoon, Harry." She greeted the proprietor with a ready smile.

"Mrs. Trevor," he returned formally. "Nice day, isn't it?"

"It's a beautiful day." She handed him the letter. "It already looks like Christmas." The snow was drifting slowly down, sparkling and pristine.

He nodded. "This all I can do for you?"

Caroline shrugged. "It is unless you can sell me a pizza. I've had the craving for a thick, cheesy pizza all week."

He chuckled and rubbed the side of his jaw. "Sorry. Can't help you there."

"That's what I figured. Oh, well." With a cheery wave, she was gone.

Paul rounded the corner of the supply store just as Caroline disappeared. "Afternoon, Harry. Was that my wife?"

"Yup, you just missed her. She came to mail a letter."

He glanced over at Caroline, but she was too far away for him to shout.

"Thick letter, too, now that I look at it. She might be needing an extra stamp. I'd best weigh it."

Paul nodded, hardly hearing the man. "She's fond of those aunts of hers."

"Her aunt has a funny name then. Larry Atkins."

The name sliced through Paul as effectively as a knife. He attempted to hide his shock and anger from Harry, but wasn't sure he'd succeeded. Without bothering to buy what he'd come for, Paul left and went back to the pumping station. He tried reasoning with himself that it was only a letter, then he recalled all the times Caroline had walked letters over to Harry, preferring to deliver them herself, claiming she needed the exercise.

His anger increased when he remembered how she'd sat at the desk across from his own at the station and vowed to find a means of escaping him. Her voice had been filled with conviction and vengeance. In his foolishness, Paul had believed her feelings had changed. He certainly hadn't expected her to be so deceitful.

"That's ridiculous," Paul said aloud. "No woman is that good an actress."

All the talk of a child. He groaned. She knew his greatest weakness. He sat at his desk and slumped forward, burying his face in his hands. He couldn't condemn her on such flimsy evidence, but he couldn't trust her either. She'd taught him that once—when she'd walked out on him with Burt Manners—but it seemed he was a slow learner.

By the time Paul arrived home that evening, he was, to all appearances, outwardly calm.

Caroline whirled around when he entered the cabin "Guess what I'm making for dinner." Her smile was brighter than the sun had been all day.

"What's that, love?"

"Pizza."

"Pizza?"

"Well, a close facsimile. I didn't have a round pan so I'm using a square one. And I didn't want to make bread dough, so I'm making do with biscuit batter. And last but not least, we didn't have any sausage so I'm using ground caribou."

"A caribou pizza?"

"How does that sound?"

"Like we'll be eating scrambled eggs later."

"Oh, ye of little faith."

Paul laughed shortly; she didn't know the half of it.

Dinner was only partially successful. To her credit, the caribou pizza wasn't bad. He managed to eat a piece and praised her ingenuity.

"What's for dinner tomorrow night? Moose Tacos?"

She laughed and promised him fried chicken.

While Caroline did the dishes, she watched Paul. He sat in the recliner with the paper resting on his lap as he stared into space. His face was so intent that she wondered what could be troubling him.

"Paul."

He shook himself from his reverie.

"Is something wrong?" she asked.

"No. I was just thinking."

"About what? You looked so pensive."

"Life." His grin was wry.

"Life?"

"It's taken an unexpected turn for us, hasn't it?" He eyed her carefully, hoping to read her heart and recognize the truth. He saw the love and devotion shining from her eyes and didn't know what to believe.

"Tanana let me watch Carl for her this afternoon," she announced, smiling. "He's growing so fast."

"You love that baby, don't you?"

"As much as if he were our own."

Tenderness wrapped its way around his heart, suffocating his doubts. He loved Caroline more than life itself. If she was playing him for a fool, then he was the happiest idiot alive. He planned to hold on to that contentment, hug it close and treasure every minute she was with him for as long as it lasted. She might dream of her precious Larry, she might even write the bastard, but it was in the curve of his arm that she slept. It was his body that filled hers and gave her pleasure. It was his name she now had and later, God willing, it would be his children she bore.

When they made love that night, it was as if a storm of passion had overtaken them. As if electricity arced between them, the current more powerful than lightning. Each caress became a fire fueled by their love.

Afterward, Caroline lay limp and drowsy in her husband's arms. Her cheeks were bright with the blush of pleasure, her breath uneven. Paul closed his eyes, wondering how he could ever have doubted her. He buried his face in her hair, savoring the fragrance, and held her against him until her breathing grew even and regular.

Caroline wasn't sure what woke her. One minute she was asleep and the next awake. It took her a moment to realize Paul wasn't asleep, either.

"Paul, what's wrong?"

"Not a thing, love."

She slipped her hand over his ribs and kissed his throat. He'd been so quiet this evening and their lovemaking had been a desperate act of passion. Paul wasn't himself and Caroline wondered what had happened. "I've failed you in some way, haven't I?"

He hesitated. "No, love, I fear I may have failed you."

"Paul, no. I'm happy, truly happy."

"Do you miss Seattle?"

"I miss my aunts," she admitted. "I wish you could meet them. And now and then I think about my friends, but there's nothing for me in Seattle now that I'm with you."

"I love you, Caroline."

She smiled and kissed the side of his mouth. He'd shown her his love in a hundred ways, but he'd never said the words. "I know."

"You're laughing at me, aren't you?" His grip on her tightened, and Caroline jerked away from him with a gasp.

"Paul, what's gotten into you?"

He held himself rigid and didn't speak for an interminable moment. "I told you I loved you and I know you were smiling."

"I...was happy." She lay on her stomach, her hands beneath her.

Another long minute passed. "I'm sorry, love. I didn't mean to frighten you."

She nodded and rolled away from him. Their happiness was shattering right before her eyes and she was powerless to stop it.

"Caroline," he said at last, reaching for her. "I talked to Harry after you were in the store today. I saw the letter you'd written to Larry Atkins."

"It's obvious you didn't read it."

"Why?"

"If you had, your reaction would be altogether different."

"Have you written him in the past?" Paul hated his jealousy. All day he'd been brooding, furious with himself and unreasonable with Caroline. If love did this to a man, he wanted no part of it, and yet he wouldn't, couldn't, give her up.

"This is my first letter to him."

"Why did you feel it was necessary to contact him now?"

"To thank him."

"What?"

"It's true. You mean, *this* is what's been bothering you?"

He didn't answer, ashamed of his behavior.

"Why didn't you ask me earlier? I would've told you all about it. I wrote Larry to let him know he'd done me a gigantic favor by standing me up at the altar."

"You told him that?"

"Not exactly in those words, but basically that's what I said."

"Why didn't you tell me you were writing him?"

Caroline expelled her breath on a nervous sigh. "To be truthful, I didn't think about it. My mistake. Are you always going to be this irrational?"

"When it comes to my wife contacting another guy, I guess I am."

"It isn't the way you're making it sound."

"I have only your word for that."

Caroline fumed, feeling insulted and angry, but rather than argue, she turned her back on him. "Good night, Paul," she grumbled. It wouldn't help matters to talk to him now. In the morning things would be better.

For two days they put the incident behind them. Their happiness was too complete to be destroyed over a silly letter and they each seemed to realize it. On the third day, Paul got home two hours before his usual time.

"You're home early." She looked up from writing Christmas cards, delighted to see her husband.

He sat at the table across from her. "I've got to fly into Fairbanks for a few days."

"Oh, Paul, Fairbanks? I can hardly wait! The first thing I'm going to do is order a real sausage pizza with extra cheese and then I'm going to shop for twelve hours nonstop. You have no idea how much I want to buy Tanana and the baby something special for Christmas. Why didn't you tell me earlier?"

"Because—"

"And you know what else I'm going to do?" She answered her own question before he had the chance, her voice animated and high-pitched. "I'm going to soak in a hot bubble bath and watch television and then I'm—"

"Caroline," he broke in gruffly, his gaze avoiding hers. "This is a business trip. I hadn't planned to bring you along."

Eight

It took a minute for the words to sink in. "You're not taking me with you?" With deliberate patience, Caroline set down the pen and pushed the Christmas cards aside. "Why?"

Paul refused to meet her probing gaze. "I've already explained that it's a business trip."

"That's not the reason and you know it." She'd thought they'd come so far, but the only one who'd moved had been her. She'd walked into his arms and been so blinded by her love she hadn't even seen the chains that bound her.

"I don't know what you're talking about."

"Like hell!"

"I go to Fairbanks every other month or so...."

"Every other month?"

"You can come with me another time."

"I want to go now."

"No!"

"Why not?" She was growing more furious by the moment.

"Because—"

"Because you saw that stupid letter to Larry and you're convinced I've made arrangements to escape. To catch a plane out of Fairbanks."

"Don't be ridiculous." But her accusation was so close to the truth that Paul's heart pounded hard against his ribs.

Caroline's smile was sarcastic. "Since

I'm your prisoner, after all, you might as well lock me in a cell."

"You're my wife!"

"I'm the woman who was forced to stay married to you. What we have isn't a marriage!" She saw him open his mouth to contradict her, then close it again. "It takes more than a piece of paper."

"Caroline, you're making too much of this."

"Yes, master," she said, gazing straight ahead, refusing to look at him. "Whatever you say, master." She bent low in a mocking bow, folding her hands in front of her.

"Caroline, stop that."

"Anything you say, master." He wanted a slave? Fine! She'd give him one. She'd speak only when spoken to, accede to his every wish, smother him with servitude.

Her unflagging calmness shocked

her. It was as though the sun had come out, revealing all the glaring imperfections of their relationship. She stared at the flaws, saddened and appalled. She'd come to love Paul and Alaska. She'd found happiness with him— only to discover it was badly marred. She was no better off now than she'd been that first week, when he'd turned her into his shadow. The only difference was that she'd grown more comfortable in her cell.

Another thought came to her and she forgot her resolve not to speak. "How… how do I know you don't have a lover in Fairbanks?"

Paul stood, pushing back the kitchen chair so suddenly it threatened to topple. "That's crazy! I can't believe you'd even think such a thing!"

"Why? I've lived with you for these past two months, so I'm well aware of your appetite for—"

"The only lover I have is you!" He shouted the words and shoved his hands inside his pants pockets.

"If you can't trust me, there's nothing that says I have to trust you." She didn't think for a minute that Paul did have another woman, but she wanted him to sample a taste of her own frustration. "The fact that you don't want me along speaks for itself. It's obvious you're hiding something from me." She arched her brows speculatively. "Another woman, no doubt."

Paul's mouth was tight. "That thought is unworthy of you."

"What else am I supposed to believe?"

His expression darkened. "I'm leaving for Fairbanks and you're staying here and that's the way it's going to be."

"Yes, master." She bowed in a sweeping, exaggerated manner.

He sighed loudly. "Are we back to that?"

She didn't answer. Instead she walked across the cabin and reached for her parka and boots. "I'm going to see Tanana unless my master demands that I remain here."

"Caroline." He stopped her just before she opened the door, but she didn't turn around and Paul knew she was fighting back tears. He felt himself go weak; he loved her and wished he could take away the pain, but it was too late to change his plans. "Never mind," he said gruffly.

Caroline left, closing the door behind her.

Paul paced the room, his emotions in conflict. Caroline was right; she'd given him everything—her love, her heart, her trust… And yet, he wasn't satisfied. He wanted more.

The cold wind cut through Caroline's

jacket as she trudged the frozen pathway that led to the Eagleclaws' cabin. She needed to get away and think. Paul had hurt her; he'd never guess the extent to which his doubts and his exclusion had pained her sensitive heart.

Tanana answered the knock at her door, looking relieved to discover it was Caroline. The baby cried pitifully in the background.

"Carl cried all night. I'm afraid he's sick."

Caroline didn't bother to take off her parka, but walked directly to the baby's side. Gently, she lifted him from the crib. His little face was red and his legs were drawn up against his stomach.

"He might have colic."

"Colic?"

"Does he cry after each feeding?"

"And before. All he does is cry."

From the young woman's obvious exhaustion, Caroline could believe it.

"Then I think you should make an appointment with the medical team for next week."

Tanana agreed with a brief nod.

"Lie down for a while and rest," Caroline said. "I'll hold Carl."

"You spoil him."

Caroline grinned and kissed the top of his small head. "I know, but let me do it, okay?"

"You'll make a good mother for Paul Trevor's sons."

Caroline quickly averted her face so her friend couldn't read her distress. She spent most of the afternoon with Tanana and the baby, leaving only when she was sure Carl would sleep and that his mother had received a few hours' rest.

"Send Thomas if you need me," she said on her way out the door.

Paul met Caroline halfway back to the cabin. His eyes held hers in a long, steady look. "I'll be leaving in a few minutes."

"Does my master wish me to carry his bags to the airstrip?"

"Caroline...don't, please."

Keeping up this charade was hard enough when her heart was breaking. "Carl has colic and poor Tanana's been up with him for two nights." She tried to cover the uncomfortable silence.

Paul's eyes caressed her. "Don't go to the airstrip. There's no need."

She lowered her gaze, already feeling herself weaken.

Walter met them and loaded Paul's suitcase onto the back of his sled. He seemed to realize that Paul and Caroline needed time alone.

"Caroline," Paul began. "You're not a prisoner." He took her in his arms and held her close, shutting his eyes to savor the feel of her against him. Their coats were so thick, holding each other was awkward and he reluctantly dropped his arms.

Caroline swallowed her anger. "When will you be back?"

"In four days, possibly five."

It seemed a lifetime, but she said nothing. His hands caressed her face with such tenderness that Caroline closed her eyes and swayed toward him. When he covered her mouth with his, her lips parted in eager welcome. The kiss was long and thorough, making her all the more aware of the seductive power he held over her senses. Of their own volition, her arms slid upward and around his neck. One kiss and he'd destroyed her resolve. Caroline didn't know whether she was more furious with Paul or with herself.

"Oh, love," he breathed against her lips. "Next time maybe you'll come with me."

Purposefully, she stepped away from

him. She was frustrated with herself for being so weak and even more so with Paul for not trusting her. "I'll be happy to go with you if I'm still here."

The shock that contorted Paul's features and narrowed his eyes caused Caroline to suck in her breath. Abruptly he turned away, marching to the airstrip without a word of farewell.

Caroline wondered what had made her say something so stupid. She regretted her sharp tongue, but Paul had hurt her and she wanted him to realize that.

"Damn!" She stamped her foot in the dry snow. If she'd hoped to build a foundation of trust, she'd just crumbled its cornerstone.

Caroline stood where she was until Paul's plane had taxied away and ascended into the gray sky. Only then did she return to the cabin, disillusioned and miserable. She was astonished by how empty the place felt. She remained standing in the middle of the living room for several minutes, hardly able to believe that in the span of a few hours, her entire world could have been jolted so badly.

That night, Caroline slept fitfully. She was too cold, then too hot. Her pillow was too flat and the mattress sagged on one side. After midnight, she admitted it wasn't the bed or the blankets. The problem was that the space beside her was empty. With a sigh, she turned and stared up at the ceiling, trying to think of ways to repair her marriage.

Paul set his suitcase on the carpeted floor of the Hotel Fairbanks. His room was adequate—a double bed, dresser, television and chair. He stared at the TV set and experienced a twinge of regret. The sensation multiplied when his gaze fell on the bathtub.

Regret hounded him. Not once in all

the weeks that Caroline had been in Gold River had she complained about the less-than-ideal living conditions. Yet she'd been denied the simplest of pleasures.

Slowly, Paul removed his parka and tossed it carelessly on the bed, then rubbed his eyes. He was determined to rush this trip so he could get back to Caroline and rebuild what his jealous doubts had destroyed.

After he'd undressed and climbed into the soft bed, Paul lay on his back, arms folded behind his head. It didn't feel right to be here without Caroline. He smiled as he recalled how quickly she'd dropped her self-imposed role of servant; she had too much fire in her to play the part with any conviction.

He thought about her being alone in the cabin, curled up and sleeping in his bed, and experienced such an overwhelming surge of desire that his body tightened and tension knotted his stomach. She often slept in that thin piece of silk her aunts had given her. Usually it rode up her slim body so that if he reached for her, his hand met warm, soft skin.

Paul inhaled sharply at the memory. Her eagerness for his lovemaking had been a surprise and a delight. She hadn't refused him once, welcoming his ardor with an enthusiasm he hadn't dared expect. He wouldn't leave her again, wouldn't take another trip unless she could join him. He planned on telling her so the minute he returned to Gold River.

Caroline woke early the next morning. As usual it was dark. The hours of daylight were becoming shorter and shorter as they approached the winter solstice. More and more of each day was spent in complete darkness. She contemplated the summer and what it would be like to have the sun shine late at night. Then she wondered if she'd be in Gold River to see it. The thought stunned her. Of course, she'd be in Gold River. This was her home now.

No sooner had she dressed and made breakfast than there was a knock at her door. Walter Thundercloud stood on the other side.

"Good morning, Walter."

He nodded politely, and stepped inside, looking a bit uneasy.

Without asking, she poured him a cup of coffee and set it on the table.

"You okay?" he asked gruffly.

"Of course I am."

"Paul asked me to check on you."

Caroline pulled out a chair and sat across from the old man. Naturally Paul would want to be sure his prisoner was in her cell, she told herself wryly. Her hands tightened on the thick mug. "I'm fine. You needn't worry about me."

Walter hesitated. "Paul's been in Gold River for several years now."

Her husband's friend seemed to be leading up to something. She nodded, hoping that was encouragement enough for him to continue.

"When he first came, he had the cabin built for privacy. The oil company had supplied his quarters, but he wanted a larger place—more homey— so he could bring his wife to live with him."

"His wife!" Caroline nearly choked on her coffee.

"Oh, the woman wasn't his wife yet. She'd only promised to be."

"I…see." Paul had been engaged! "What happened?"

"He never told me, but one day he got a letter and after he read it, Paul left the station and got sick drunk. He never mentioned her name again."

Nor had he mentioned the woman to Caroline. The heat of jealous anger blossomed in her cheeks. The night of her arrival, she'd spilled her guts about Larry. Apparently, Paul had gone through a similar experience and hadn't bothered to tell her. Talk about trust!

"For many months, Paul was angry. He worked too hard, not sleeping some nights. He scowled and snapped and drank more than he should."

"He didn't leave Gold River and try to work things out with this woman?"

"No."

Caroline took another sip of her coffee, somehow not surprised. He had an overabundance of pride, often to his own detriment. "Why are you telling me this?"

"For the first time since Paul moved to Gold River, he smiles every day. He laughs. Before my eyes I've seen him change. He's happy now. These changes began when you came here."

So Walter wanted to reassure her. She smiled softly and stared at her coffee. His words only proved how little she knew of the man who was her husband.

"What made Paul decide to get married now?"

Walter shrugged. "He wants a family."

She nodded. Tanana had told her that, too.

"He loves you," Walter continued. "I don't believe Paul ever thought he'd be fortunate enough to find a woman as good as you. He put the ad in the paper because he was lonely."

"But why did he advertise for a wife? Surely there were women who'd want to marry him. Someone in Fairbanks, maybe?"

Walter added sugar to his coffee, stirring it a long time. "You'll have to ask him that."

Alarm turned her blood cold. "He has a woman in Fairbanks?"

Walter chuckled and shook his head. "He advertised for a bride because he didn't have time to properly date someone and build a relationship by the usual means. I also think he was afraid the same thing would happen to him a second time and she'd change her mind."

No wonder he'd been so insistent that they stay married. "Why is a child so important to Paul?"

"I suppose because he didn't have a family when he was growing up."

This was another shock to Caroline. Paul had spoken only briefly about his background. He'd been raised somewhere in Texas. As far as she knew, he hadn't contacted his parents about their marriage and now that she considered it, Paul seemed to change the subject whenever she asked about his childhood.

The faded eyes brightened. "I'm not telling you these things to stir up trouble." The old man paused. "I can see that most of what I've said has been a shock. Paul might not appreciate my loose tongue, but I felt you should know that he's gone through some hard times. You've been good for him."

"Our relationship is still on rocky ground."

"I can see that. I was surprised he didn't take you to Fairbanks and when I mentioned it, he nearly bit my head off."

"You were right when you guessed that I love him."

"He feels the same way. He'd move heaven and earth to see that you were happy. He—"

An abrupt knock sounded, drawing their attention to the front door. Thomas Eagleclaw stepped in without waiting for an invitation. His eyes were frightened. "Mrs. Paul, please come."

"What is it?"

"Tanana and the baby are sick."

As Walter and Thomas spoke in low voices, Caroline stood and reached for her coat. Momentarily, her gaze collided with Walter's. The older man pulled on his parka, as well, and followed her to the Eagleclaws' cabin. Even before they arrived at the small log structure, Caroline had a premonition of disaster.

The baby lay in his crib, hardly moving. He stared at her with wide eyes and when Caroline felt his skin, he was burning up with fever. "How long has he been like this?"

"Apparently Tanana's been ill, too." Walter answered for the young man.

"Why didn't you let me know?" Caroline asked Thomas.

"Tanana probably told him not to.

She didn't want to trouble you," Walter whispered, standing at Caroline's side.

"But Carl's very sick."

"Mary Finefeather has a fever," Thomas announced.

"Mary, too?"

Caroline turned to Walter. "I'll do what I can here and meet you at Mary's. We may need to get help."

Walter nodded and left.

Tanana's face felt hot, and the girl whimpered softly when Caroline tried to talk to her.

The young husband stood stiffly by the bedside. "She's much worse this morning."

"Oh, Thomas, I wish you'd come for me," Caroline said, more sharply than she intended.

The young man looked guiltily at the floor.

"How are you feeling?"

He shrugged, still not looking at her.

Caroline pressed the back of her hand to his forehead and shook her head. "Get into bed and I'll be back when I can."

Although she tried to stay calm, her heart was racing. She hurried from the Eagleclaws' to Mary's. Once there, Caroline discovered that the older woman's symptoms were similar to Tanana's and the baby's.

"Walter, contact the Public Health Department and see if they can fly in some help. I don't know what we've got here, but I don't like the looks of it."

Walter's eyes met hers. "In the winter of 1979 we lost twelve to the fever."

"We're not going to lose anyone this time. Now hurry!"

After his meeting with the oil company engineers, Paul paused on the sidewalk outside the jewelry store to study the diamond rings on display.

It'd never occurred to him to ask Caroline if she wanted a diamond. She wore the simple gold band he'd given her and hadn't asked for anything more. Now he wondered if she was disappointed with the simplicity of the ring.

He thought about the gifts he'd already purchased and realized he'd probably need to buy another suitcase to haul them all back to Gold River. He smiled at the thought. He'd bought her everything she'd ever mentioned wanting and, in addition, purchased gifts for Tanana and the baby, knowing Caroline had wanted to get them something special. Paul was trying to make up to her for excluding her from this trip. Never again would he leave her behind. He decided he'd buy her a ring and save it for Christmas. Everything else he'd give her when he got home.

Never had he been more anxious to return to Gold River.

* * *

The Public Health Department flew in a doctor and two nurses that same afternoon. The community meeting hall served as a makeshift hospital and the sickest were brought there. Tanana, the baby and Mary Finefeather had been the first to become seriously ill. Others soon followed. Within two days, Caroline and the medical staff were tending twenty-five patients. The following day it was thirty, then thirty-five.

"How long has it been since you slept?" Dr. Mather asked Caroline on the third day.

Her smile was weak. "I forget."

"That's what I thought. Go get some rest, and that's an order."

She shook her head. She couldn't leave when so many were sick and more arrived every hour. The other staff members had rested intermittently. "I'm fine."

"If you don't do as I say, you'll be sick next."

"I'm not leaving."

"Stubborn woman." But his eyes spoke of admiration.

Later that day, Walter brought her something to eat and forced her to sit down. "I think I should contact Paul."

"Don't." She placed her hand on his forearm and silently pleaded with him. "He'd only worry."

"He should worry. You're working yourself into an early grave."

"I'm totally healthy."

"You won't be if you go on like this."

Walter gave her one of his looks and Caroline sighed. "All right, we'll compromise. I'll go lie down in a few minutes, but I'll have someone wake me after an hour."

Mary Finefeather died early the next morning. Caroline stood at Dr. Mather's side as he pulled the sheet over the woman's face, relaxed now in death. Tears burned Caroline's eyes, but she dared not let them flow. So many needed her; she had to be strong.

"Are you doing okay?" the doctor asked.

"I think so," Caroline answered in a strangled voice. "What about the baby?" She'd held Carl for most of the night. He was so weak, too weak even to cry. He'd lain limp in her arms, barely moving.

The doctor hesitated. "It doesn't look good. If he lasts through the day, then his chances will improve."

The floor pitched beneath her feet. She'd known it herself, but had been afraid to admit it. "And his mother?"

"She's young and strong. She should make it."

"Anyone else?"

"Two others look serious."

Caroline bit the inside of her cheek and followed him to the next bed.

* * *

At the end of the fourth day, his meetings finished and his shopping done, Paul returned to the hotel, packed his bags and checked out. He felt as anxious as a kid awaiting the end of school. He was going home to Gold River, home to Caroline. After a short trip to a pizza parlor, the taxi delivered him to the airport. If Burt Manners was late, Paul swore he'd have his hide.

The pilot was waiting for Paul at the designated area inside the terminal. Burt rose to his feet as Paul approached.

"I've got bad news for you," he said, frowning as he eyed the pizza box.

"What's that?"

"We aren't going to be able to fly into Gold River."

"Why not?" Frustration made Paul tighten his grip around the handle of his bag.

"A white-out."

"Damn!" Paul expelled the word viciously. A white-out was dangerous enough to put the finest, most experienced pilot on edge. Visibility plummeted to zero, and flying was impossible. The condition could last for days.

"There's nothing more you can do." Dr. Mather spoke gently to Caroline and attempted to remove the lifeless four-year-old child from her arms.

"No, please," she whispered, bringing the still body closer to her own. "Let me hold her for a few more minutes. I…I just want to say goodbye."

The doctor stepped aside and waited.

Caroline brushed the hair from the sweet face and kissed the smooth brow, rocking her to and fro, singing the little girl a lullaby she'd never hear. Anna was dead and Caroline was sure Carl was next. Tears rained unchecked down her cheeks. She took a moment to compose herself, then handed the child to the doctor. "I'll tell her mother."

A week after Paul had left Gold River, he returned. Walter was at the airstrip waiting for him when the plane taxied to a standstill. One look at the other man's troubled frown and sad eyes, and Paul knew something was terribly wrong.

"What is it?"

"The fever came. Five are dead."

Fear closed Paul's throat. "Caroline?"

"She's been working for days without sleep. Thank God you're back."

"Take me to her."

By the time Paul reached the meeting hall, his heart was pounding. Rarely had he moved more quickly. If anything happened to Caroline, he'd blame himself. He'd left her, abandoned her to some unspeakable fate. He stopped in the doorway, appalled at the scene.

Stretchers littered the floor, children crying, staff moving from one patient to another.

It took him a moment to find Caroline. She was bent over an old woman, lifting the weary head and helping her sip liquid through a straw. Caroline looked frail, and when she straightened, she staggered and nearly fell backward.

Paul was at her side instantly. She turned and looked at him as though he were a stranger.

"I'm getting you out of here," Paul said, furious that she'd worked herself into this condition and no one had stopped her.

"No, please," she said in a voice so weak it quavered. "I'm fine." With that, she promptly fainted.

Paul caught her before she hit the floor.

Nine

Caroline struggled to open her eyes. The lids felt incredibly heavy. She discovered Paul sleeping awkwardly in a kitchen chair by her bed. She realized he must have brought her home. He was slouched so that his head rested against the back. One arm hugged his ribs and the other hung loosely at his side. Caroline blinked. Paul looked terrible; his clothes were wrinkled, his shirt pulled out from the waistband and half-unbuttoned.

"Paul?" she whispered, having difficulty finding her voice. She forced herself to swallow. When Paul didn't respond, Caroline raised her hand and tugged at his shirttail.

His eyes flew open and he bolted upright. "Caroline? You're awake!" He rose to his feet and shook the unkempt hair from his face, staring down at her. "How do you feel?"

The past week suddenly returned to haunt her. She thought of Mary Finefeather and Anna, the bubbly four-year-old. An overwhelming sadness at the loss of her friends brought stinging tears to her eyes.

"Carl?" She managed to squeeze the name of the baby from her throat.

"He's improving and so is Tanana."

"Good." Caroline closed her eyes because sleep was preferable to the memories.

When she awakened again, Paul was sitting in the chair beside their bed.

Only this time his elbows were resting on his knees, his face buried in his hands. She must have made a sound because he slowly lifted his head.

"How long have I been asleep?" she asked.

"Almost twenty-four hours."

She arched her eyebrows in surprise. "Did I catch the fever?"

"The doctor said it was exhaustion." Paul stood and poured a glass of water and supported her so she could sip from it. When she'd finished, he lowered her back to the bed.

Caroline turned her face away so she wouldn't have to watch his expression. "I want to go home."

"Caroline, love, you are home."

Her eyes drifted shut. She hadn't thought it would be easy.

"Caroline, I know you're upset, but you'll feel different later. I promise you will."

Despite her resolve not to cry, tears coursed down her cheeks. "I hate Alaska. I want to go where death doesn't...doesn't come with the dark, where I can hear children laugh and smell flowers again." People had died here—people she'd loved, people she'd come to care about. Friends. Children. Babies. The marriage she'd worked so hard to build wasn't a real one. The only thing that held it together was Paul's indomitable pride—he wasn't going to let her go after he'd already lost one woman.

"You don't know what you're saying," he told her, discounting her words as he reached for her hand.

"I want to go home. To Seattle."

He released her hand and she heard him stalk to the other side of the room. "I'll fix you something to eat."

Alone now, Caroline pushed back the covers, then carefully sat up. The room spun and teetered, but she gripped the headboard and gradually everything righted itself.

Suddenly she felt terribly hungry. When Paul returned, carrying a tray of tea, toast and scrambled eggs, she didn't even consider refusing it.

He piled her pillows against the headboard and set the tray on her lap. When it looked as though he meant to feed her, Caroline stopped him with a gesture

"I can do it."

He nodded and sat back in the chair. "Walter said you nearly killed yourself. You wouldn't leave or rest or eat. Why did you push yourself like that, love?" He paused and watched her lift the fork to her mouth in a deliberate movement. "He told me about little Anna dying in your arms."

Caroline chewed slowly, but not by choice; even eating required energy. She didn't want to talk about Anna, the fever or anything else. She didn't answer Paul's questions because she couldn't explain to him something she didn't fully understand herself. In some incomprehensible way, she felt responsible for the people in Gold River. They were her friends, her family, and she'd let them down.

"I can't tell you how bad I feel that I left you here to deal with—"

"Why didn't you mention her?"

Paul gave her an odd look. "Mention who?"

She glared at him. "You *know* who."

"Don't tell me we're going through this again. Should I duck to avoid the salt and pepper shakers?" Mockingly he held up his hands, his eyes twinkling.

For a moment, Caroline was furious enough to hurl something at him, but that required more energy than she had.

"Caroline, love…"

"I'm not your love," she said heatedly.

Paul chuckled. "You can't honestly mean that after the last few weeks."

"Correction," she said bitterly. "I'm not your *first* love."

Paul went still and his eyes narrowed. "All right, what did you find?"

"Find?" Caroline discovered she was shaking. "Find? Do you mean to tell me you've got…memorabilia stored in this cabin from that…that other woman?"

"Caroline, settle down…."

"Oh-h-h." It took all her restraint not to fling a leftover piece of toast at him. He must have noticed the temptation because he quickly took the tray from her lap and returned it to the kitchen.

While he was gone, Caroline lay back down and tried to compose her thoughts. He'd loved another woman so much that it had taken him years to commit himself to a new relationship. Caroline was simply filling some other woman's place in his life. What bothered her most was that he'd never told her about this previous lover. The more she learned, the more imperative it became to leave.

He entered the bedroom again, his steps hesitant. He'd slipped the tips of his fingers in the back pockets of his jeans. "This isn't the time to talk about Diane. When you're feeling better, I'll tell you everything you want to know."

"Diane," Caroline repeated, vowing to hate every woman with that name. An eerie calm came over her as she raised her eyes to meet Paul's. "This... Diane didn't happen to be blond, blue-eyed and about five-five, did she?"

Paul looked stunned. "You knew her?"

"You idiot, that's me!" She grabbed a pillow and heaved it at him with all her strength. She was so weak it didn't even make it to the end of the bed.

Paul shook his head. "Love, listen, I know what this sounds like."

"Get out!"

"Caroline…"

"I'm sure the doctor told you I should remain calm. The very sight of you boils my blood, so kindly leave before there's cardiovascular damage!"

He advanced toward her and Caroline scrambled to her knees and reached for the glass of water. "You take one more step and you'll be wearing this!"

Exasperated, Paul swore under his breath. "How you could be so utterly unreasonable is beyond me."

"Unreasonable!" She lifted the tumbler and brought back her arm, making the threat more real. That persuaded him to exit the room. Once he'd gone, Caroline curled up in a tight ball, shaking with fury. Not only hadn't he told her about Diane, but he'd chosen *her* because she obviously resembled the other woman. He'd told her often enough that as soon as he'd seen her picture, he'd known. Sure he'd known! She was a duplicate of the woman he'd once loved.... And probably still did.

Caroline escaped into a deep, blissful slumber. When she awakened, she felt stronger and, although she was a bit shaky on her feet, she managed to dress and pull the suitcase from beneath the bed. Her hands trembled as she neatly folded and packed each garment.

"What are you doing?" Paul asked from behind her.

Caroline stiffened. "What I should've done weeks ago. Leaving Gold River. Leaving Alaska. Leaving you."

He didn't say anything for a long, tense moment. "I realize things are a bit unsettled between us," he finally muttered, "but we'll work it out."

"Unsettled. You call this *unsettled?* Well, I've got news for you, Paul Trevor.

Things are more than just unsettled. I want out. O-U-T. Out!"

"I won't agree to a divorce."

"Fine, we'll stay married if that's what you want. We'll have the ideal marriage—I'll be in Seattle and you can live here. No more arguing. No more disagreements. No more Scrabble." Frantically, she stacked her sweaters in the open suitcase. "Believe me, after this experience I have no desire to involve myself with another man ever again."

"Caroline—"

"I'll tell you one thing I'm grateful for, though," she said, interrupting him. "You taught me a lot about myself. Here I was, playing Clara Barton to an entire town as if I were some heroine, dispensing medical knowledge and good will. But…but people *died*."

"Caroline—"

"I even fooled myself into thinking

you and I could make a go of this marriage. I thought, 'Paul Trevor's a good man. Better than most. Fair. Kind. Tender.' I'll admit the events leading up to our marriage were bizarre to say the least, but I was ready to stick it out and make the best of the situation. Things could've been worse—I could've married Larry." She laughed without amusement.

His hands settled on her shoulders and he attempted to turn her around, but Caroline wouldn't let him. "Please don't touch me." His touch was warm and gentle, and she couldn't resist him. Her eyes filled with tears and Paul swam in and out of her vision as she backed away from him.

"I can't let you go, love," he said softly.

"You don't have any choice."

"Caroline, give it a week. You're distraught now, but in a few days, I promise you'll feel differently."

"No," she sobbed, jerking her head back and forth. "I can't stay another day. Please, I need to get out of here."

"Let me hold you for just a minute."

"No." But she didn't fight him when he reached for her and brought her into the circle of his arms.

"I know, love," he whispered. "I know." He felt his heart catch at the anguish in her tormented expression. She hid her face in his shirt and wept, her shoulders shaking with such force that Paul braced his feet to hold her securely.

"Anna—she died in my arms," she wailed.

"I know, love, I know." His hand smoothed her hair in long, even strokes. Regret cut though him. He'd abandoned her to face the crisis alone, never dreaming anything like this would happen, thinking only of himself. He'd been so selfish. And despite the way she'd disparaged her own efforts, she *had* been a heroine.

When her tears were spent, Caroline raised her head and wiped her face. Paul's shirt bore evidence of her crying and she guiltily tried to rub away the tear stains.

His hand stopped hers and he tenderly brought her palm to his mouth. He kissed it while his eyes held hers. She didn't want him to be so gentle; she wanted to hate him so she could leave and never look back.

"Please don't," she pleaded weakly.

Paul released her hand.

"Caroline," he said seriously. "You can't go."

"Why not? Nothing binds us except a piece of paper." He flinched at her words and she regretted hurting him.

"I love you," he whispered.

Knotting her hands into fists, she

raised her chin a fraction. "Did you love Diane, too?"

Paul's face seemed to lose its color.

"Did you?" she cried.

"Yes."

Caroline pressed her advantage. "You let *her* go. You didn't go after her and force her to marry you and live on this frozen chunk of ice. All I'm asking for is the same consideration."

"You don't know—"

"I do. I know everything I need to know about Alaska and Gold River. I know I can't live here anymore. I know I can't look you in the face and feel I'm your wife and you're my husband. I know I can't bear any more pain. Please, Paul, let me go home." She was weeping again, almost uncontrollably.

Paul advanced a step toward her. "You'll feel better tomorrow," he said again, then turned and left the room.

Caroline slumped on the bed and

wept until her eyes burned and there were no more tears. Spent, she fell asleep, only to wake in a dark, shadowless room. Paul had placed a blanket over her shoulders. She sat up and brushed the unruly mass of hair from her face.

Instantly, Paul stood in the doorway. "You're awake."

"Yes, master."

He sighed, but said nothing more.

"I've fixed you something to eat. Would you like to come out here or would you rather I brought it in to you?"

"Whatever my master wishes."

He clenched his fists. "It'll be on the table when you're ready."

"Thank you, master." Her words were spoken in a sarcastic monotone.

Patience, Paul told himself. That was the key. Caroline had been through a traumatic experience that had mentally and physically exhausted her. She needed to know she was loved and that he'd be there to protect her. For the hundredth time, he cursed himself for having left her while he'd gone off to Fairbanks.

He ladled out a bowl of vegetable soup and set it on the table, along with thick slices of sourdough bread. Next he poured her a tall glass of milk.

While he was in the kitchen, Caroline changed clothes and brushed her teeth and hair. She looked a sight; it was a wonder Paul hadn't leapt at the chance to be rid of her.

Paul glanced up expectantly when she entered the room and pulled out a kitchen chair for her. Caroline sat down, staring at the meal. Although it smelled delicious, she had no appetite.

Her lack of interest must have been obvious because Paul spoke sharply. "Eat, Caroline."

"I...I can't."

"Try."

"I want to go home."

Paul's fists were so tight his fingers ached. *Patience,* he reminded himself—and she'd only been awake a few hours.

He took the chair across from her and watched her as she methodically lifted the spoon to her mouth. "I brought you some things from Fairbanks. Would you like to see them?" he coaxed.

She tried to smile, but all she could think about was Seattle and her two aunts and the life she'd inadvertently left behind. A life of comfort and security she suddenly, desperately, missed. There was too much pain in Gold River. "Will you let me go home if I do?"

He felt a muscle leap in his temple, but didn't respond. He stood, opened the closet door and brought her an armful of packages.

"Go ahead and open them," he said, then changed his mind. "No. You eat,

I'll open them for you." From the first package, he produced a bottle of expensive perfume, a brand she'd once mentioned. He smiled at her, anticipating her delight.

Caroline swallowed down her surprise. He could be so loving and she didn't want him to be. Not now, when all she could think about was leaving him.

"Well?"

"It's very nice. Thank you, master."

Paul had had it. He shot to his feet. "Don't ever call me your master again!"

"Yes."

"I wish you'd stop this silly game."

"Will you let me go home if I do?" Caroline asked and took another spoonful of soup.

Paul ignored the question. From the second package he withdrew a huge teddy bear and was pleased when she paused, the spoon halfway to her mouth.

"For Carl," he explained. "You said you wanted something special for him. I thought we'd save it for Christmas."

She nodded and recalled how close they'd come to losing the baby. Tears filled her eyes.

Paul turned the bear over. "You push this button in the back and Mr. Bear actually talks."

Caroline's nod was nearly imperceptible.

"Would you like to see what I got Tanana?"

"Not now…please." She looked straight ahead, feeling dizzy and weak. Setting the spoon back on the table she closed her eyes. "Would it be all right if I lay down for a minute?"

"Of course." He moved to her side and slipped an arm around her waist as he guided her back to the bedroom. The suitcase was open on the bed. Paul moved it and put it on the floor.

Caroline felt sluggish and tired. "Do I really look like her?"

"Her? You mean Diane?"

Caroline nodded.

"I suppose there's a certain resemblance, but it's superficial."

"Why didn't you tell me about her?"

"It's a long story. Too long and complicated for right now."

"And you think my involvement with Larry *wasn't* long and complicated?"

Paul sighed and closed the lid of her suitcase. "The two aren't comparable."

"Then there's your family…"

Paul went tense. "Who told you about my family?"

"We're married," she said sadly, "and yet you hide your life from me."

"I have no family, Caroline. I was raised in a series of foster homes."

"So you're willing to tell me about your childhood, but not Diane. I think I know why."

Irritated, Paul shook his head, his mouth pinched and white. "I love you."

"Then let me go back to Seattle," she said.

"Please don't ask me that again. Give this—us—a chance."

"Yes, master," she said dully.

Paul groaned and slammed the door.

If Paul thought Caroline would forget her quest to return to Seattle, he was wrong. For two days, she sat in the cabin, listless and lethargic, gazing into space. She never spoke unless spoken to and answered his questions with as few words as possible. She wore her unhappiness like a cloak that smothered her natural exuberance.

He tried to draw her out, tried reasoning with her. Nothing helped. By the time they climbed into bed at night, he was so frustrated with her that any desire for lovemaking was destroyed.

He longed to hold her, yearned to feel her body close to his, but each time he reached for her, she froze.

She didn't talk about Seattle again. But her suitcase remained packed and ready, a constant reminder of how eager she was to leave him. He placed it back under the bed once, but she immediately pulled it out and set it by the front door. He didn't move it after that.

Every morning Paul promised himself that Caroline would be better, but nothing seemed to change. He had to find a way to reach her and was quickly running out of ideas.

But today, he vowed, would be different. He had a plan.

After dinner that evening, Paul sat in his recliner, reading the Fairbanks paper. His mind whirled with thoughts of seduction; he missed Caroline; he missed having his warm, loving wife in his arms. It had been nearly two weeks since they'd made love and if anything could shatter the barriers she'd built against him, it was their lovemaking. He smiled, content for the first time in days.

"Caroline."

She turned to him, her eyes blank. "Yes?"

"Dinner was very good tonight."

"Thank you."

"Would you come here a minute, please?"

She walked toward him with small, measured steps, refusing to meet his eyes, and paused directly in front of his chair.

"Sit on my lap."

Caroline hesitated, but did as he requested.

His hand massaged the tense muscles of her back. "Relax," he whispered.

Caroline found it impossible to do so, but said nothing.

"Okay, put your hands on my shoulders."

She did that, too, with a fair amount of reluctance.

"Now kiss me."

Her eyes narrowed as she recognized his game.

"You're so fond of calling me 'master,' I thought you might need a little direction."

She didn't move.

"Just one kiss, love?"

Lightly, she rested her hands on his shoulders and leaned forward.

"Now kiss me...."

Caroline stared at him blankly, then touched her mouth to his.

"No, a *real* kiss."

She brushed her closed mouth over his in the briefest of contacts.

"Come on, Caroline. It'll be Christmas soon, and even a grinch could do better than that."

With the tip of her tongue, she moistened her lips and slanted her head to press her mouth over his. She felt as if this was all a dream, as if it wasn't really happening.

The kiss was routine. Paul wove her hair around his fingers, placing his hand against the back of her head, holding her to him. His warmth seemed to reach her heart and Caroline felt herself soften.

"I've missed your kisses, my love." His eyes held hers. "I've missed everything about you."

Caroline couldn't seem to tear her gaze from his.

"Kiss me again—oh, Caroline, you taste so good."

He tasted wonderful, too. She settled her mouth over his, and with a sigh, she surrendered.

He continued to kiss her with an urgency that quickly became an all-consuming passion. She felt weak, spent. Her arms clung to Paul and when he ran his hand along the inside of her thigh, she squirmed, craving more and more of him. Her fingers shook almost uncontrollably as she pulled the shirt-tail from his waistband and rubbed her palms over his chest.

"I want you," he whispered.

Somehow those words permeated the fog of desire when the others hadn't. With a soft moan, she lifted her head to stare at him with tear-filled eyes.

"Love?" He reached for her and she moved away as though he held a gun in his hand.

"Paul, I can't live here anymore. It hurts too much. Please don't make me stay."

His face lost all color. He could see it was pointless to reason with her and shook his head in defeat. "Alaska is my home."

"But it isn't mine."

"You'll get over this," he told her.

"I *can't*...I won't. I tried, Paul, I honestly tried."

He was silent for so long that she wondered if he was going to speak again. "I won't come after you, Caroline. I didn't with Diane and I won't with you."

She nodded numbly. "I understand."

He clenched his fists at his sides. "I give up. I won't keep you against your will."

Tears streaked her face and when she spoke, her voice was low and hoarse. "Thank you."

"Shall I arrange for the divorce or would you rather do it yourself?"

Ten

"Oh, Sister," Ethel Myers said with a worried frown, "I don't think the brew will help dear Caroline this time."

"We must deliberate on this, and you know as well as I do that we do it so much better with Father's brew." Mabel Myers carefully poured two steaming cups of the spiked tea and handed one to her younger sister. Soft Christmas music was punctuated by the clinking of china.

"Poor Caroline."

Mabel placed the dainty cup to her

lips, paused and sighed. "She sounded so happy in her letters."

"And she tries so hard to hide her unhappiness now."

"Paul Trevor must be a terrible beast to have treated her so—"

"He isn't, Aunt Mabel," Caroline said from the archway of her aunts' parlor. "He's a wonderful man. Good, kind, generous."

Ethel reached for another porcelain cup. "Tea, dear?"

"Not me," Caroline said with a grin, recalling the last time she'd sampled her great-grandfather's brew. Before she'd known it, she'd ended up married to Paul Trevor— and in his bed.

"If he wasn't a beast, dear, why did you leave him?"

Caroline took a seat on the thick brocade sofa and shrugged. "For the wrong reasons, I suppose."

"The wrong reasons?" Ethel echoed,

and the two older women exchanged meaningful glances.

"Then, dear, perhaps you should go back."

Caroline dropped her gaze to her lap. "I can't."

"Can't?" Mabel repeated. "Whyever not?"

"There was another woman...."

"With him?" Ethel sounded shocked. "Why, that's indecent. He *is* a beast."

"He loved a woman named Diane a long time ago," Caroline corrected hurriedly. "He never actually told me about her, but when he gave me the ticket home, he said he didn't go after Diane and he wasn't coming after me."

Mabel put her hand on Caroline's in a comforting gesture. "Do you love him, dear?"

Caroline nodded again. "Very much."

"Then you must go to him."

Her two aunts made it sound so easy.

Every day since she got home, Caroline had thought of Paul. He'd been right. Time had healed her, and she'd reconciled herself to the shock of losing her friends to the fever. She'd been distraught; the people who'd died were more than patients. They'd been friends—part of her Alaskan family. Each one had touched her in a special way.

"Go to him?" Caroline repeated. "No, I can't."

"No?" both sisters exclaimed.

"If he loved me enough, he'd come to me. I need that, although I don't expect anyone else to understand the reasons."

The doorbell chimed and Caroline stood. "That must be Larry. We're going to a movie."

"Have a good time, dear."

"Oh yes, dear, have a good time."

No sooner had the front door closed than Ethel glanced at her sister, her eyes twinkling with mischief. "Shall I get the stationery or will you?"

"Hi." Larry kissed Caroline lightly on the forehead. "At least you've got some color in your face tonight."

"Thank you," she said, and laughed. Leave it to Larry to remind her that she'd been pale and sickly for weeks. "And you're looking handsome, as usual." It frightened her now to think that they'd almost married. Larry would make some woman a wonderful husband, but Caroline wasn't that woman.

"Is there any movie you'd like to see?" he asked.

"You choose." Their tastes were so different that anything she suggested would only be grounds for a lively discussion.

"There's a new musical comedy at the Fifth Avenue. Some kind of Christmas story."

His choice surprised Caroline. He wasn't really interested in musicals, preferring action movies, the more violent the better.

"Is that okay?"

Caroline looked up at him and had to blink back tears. She hadn't cried since she'd returned to Seattle. Tears were useless now. She was home and everything was supposed to be good. Only it wasn't, because Paul wasn't there to share it with her. They might have begun their marriage at a disadvantage but she'd grown to love him. And she loved his small Alaskan town, more than she would ever have believed. She'd been a fool to leave him and even more of one not to acknowledge her mistake and go back.

"I've said something to upset you?" Larry asked anxiously. "I'm sorry." His kindness only made her weep louder.

"Caroline?"

"Paul liked musicals," she explained, sniffling. "He can't sing, but that didn't stop him from belting out songs at top volume."

"You really liked this guy, didn't you?"

"He was the only man I ever met who could beat me at Scrabble."

"He beat you at Scrabble?" Even Larry sounded impressed. "As far as I can see, you two were meant for each other. Now, when are you going to admit it?"

"Never," she said and an incredible sadness came over her.

Ethel Myers sat in front of the ancient typewriter—no computers for them!—and glanced at her sibling. "Pour me another cup of tea, will you, Sister?"

"Certainly, Sister."

They looked at each other and giggled like schoolgirls.

"Caroline must never know."

"Oh, no. Caroline would definitely not approve."

"Read the letter again, Sister."

Ethel picked up the single sheet of paper and sighed. "My darling Paul," she said in a breathless whisper, as though she were an actress practicing her lines. "I feel you should know that I find myself with child. Your loving wife, Caroline."

"Excellent. Excellent."

"We'll put it in the mail first thing tomorrow."

"More tea, Sister?"

Ethel giggled and held out her cup. "Indeed."

A few days later, Caroline lay on her bed and finally admitted there was no hope. Paul wasn't coming for her. He'd told her he wouldn't, so it shouldn't be any great shock, but despite that, she'd hoped he would. If he loved her, he would have forsaken his pride and come to Seattle. So much for dreams.

She turned onto her side. Surely he realized she was waiting for him. She needed proof of his love—proof that she was more important to him than Diane had ever been. More important than his pride. She was his wife, his love. He'd told her so countless times.

Caroline sighed and closed her eyes. She missed baby Carl and Tanana and their long talks. She missed the women of the village, missed knitting the "authentic" sweaters for tourists. She missed the dusk at noon and the nonstop snow and even the unrelenting cold.

Most of all she missed Paul. He might have been able to live without her, but she was wilting away for lack of him.

With the realization that Paul's pride would keep him in Alaska came an unpleasant insight; it was up to her to swallow her own pride and go to him.

Within twenty minutes, her luggage was packed. She'd waited long enough; another day was intolerable. She'd go to him. She hated the thought of not being here to share Christmas with her aunts, but her love for Paul was too strong to give her peace.

"Are you going someplace, dear?" Aunt Mabel asked as Caroline descended the stairs, a suitcase in each hand.

"Alaska."

"Alaska?" Mabel cried, as though Caroline had said outer space.

Immediately Ethel appeared and Mabel cast a stricken gaze toward her sister. "Caroline says she's going to Alaska!"

"But she can't!"

"I can't?" Perplexed, Caroline glanced

from one addled face to the other. Only last week they'd suggested she return.

"Oh, dear, this is a problem."

Ethel looked uncomfortable. "Perhaps we should tell her, Sister."

"Perhaps we should."

Caroline knew her lovable and eccentric aunts well enough to figure out that they'd been plotting again. "I think you'd better start at the beginning," she said in a resigned voice.

Ten minutes later, after hearing all the details, Caroline accepted a cup of the special tea. She needed it. "Paul will come," she murmured. If he believed she was pregnant he'd certainly show up.

"He'll come here and then you'll be happy. Isn't that right, dear?"

Her aunts gave her a look of such innocence, she couldn't disillusion them. "Right," Caroline said weakly.

"You were going back to him," Ethel pointed out.

"Yes." But this was different. At least if she returned to Gold River, Paul would have his pride intact. But now, he'd realize he'd been tricked again.

"You're not unhappy, are you, dear?" Mabel asked softly.

"I'm happy," she replied. "Very happy."

Nodding with satisfaction, her aunts brought the teapot back to the kitchen while Caroline remained in the room off the entry that her aunts insisted on calling the parlor. The doorbell gave a musical chime and, still bemused from the tea and her aunts' schemes, Caroline rose to answer it.

The man who stood outside was tall and well-built. Attractive. Caroline glanced up at him expectantly and blinked, finding him vaguely familiar.

"Caroline, I know…"

"Paul?" She widened her eyes and felt her mouth drop open. It was Paul, but without a beard. Good grief, he was handsome! Instinctively, she lifted her hand to his clean-shaven face and ran the tips of her fingers over the lean, square jaw.

"May I come in?"

For a moment, Caroline was too shocked to react. "Oh, of course. I'm sorry." Hurriedly, she stepped aside so he could enter the Victorian house, then led him into the parlor with its beautifully decorated Christmas tree. "Please sit down."

He wore gray slacks, the Irish cable knit sweater she'd made for him and a thin jacket. Everyone else in Seattle was wearing wool coats and mufflers and claiming it was the coldest winter in fifty years.

"How are you, Caroline?"

She was starving for the sight of

him and couldn't take her eyes off his smooth jaw. "Fine," she said absently. Then she remembered what her aunts had told him and frowned. She'd have to tell him the truth, which would no doubt disappoint him. "How are you?" she asked, stalling for time.

"Fine."

Having forgotten her manners once, Caroline quickly tried to reverse her earlier lack of welcome. "Would you like some tea?"

"Coffee, if you have it." He paused to look at the portraits of her aunts on the mantel and added, "Just plain coffee."

"But you drank your coffee with cream before."

"I meant with cream. It's the other, uh, additions I'm hoping to avoid."

Her bewilderment must have shown in her eyes. "I don't want any of your aunts' brew."

"Oh, of course."

Caroline rushed into the kitchen and brought back a cup of coffee for Paul and a glass of milk for herself. Her aunts joined her and when the three of them entered the room, Paul stood.

"You must be Ethel and Mabel," he said politely.

They nodded in unison.

"He's even more handsome in person, don't you think, Sister?" Mabel trilled.

"Oh, very definitely."

"Caroline," Paul murmured when the two older women showed no signs of leaving the parlor. "Could we go someplace and talk?"

"Oh, do go, dear," Ethel encouraged with a broad grin.

"Someplace *private*," Mabel whispered, and the way she said it suggested a hotel room. Even Caroline blushed.

Paul escorted her to the car, a rental, and opened the passenger door for her. She couldn't stop staring at him. He looked so different—compelling, forthright, determined.

Once she was seated, he ran his hand over the side of his face. "I feel naked without it."

"Why…why did you shave?"

He gave her an odd look. "For you."

"Me?"

"You once said you refused to stay married to a man whose face you couldn't see."

Caroline remembered his response, too. He'd told her to get used to his beard because it was nature's protection from the Alaskan winter. He'd adamantly refused to shave then, but he'd done it now because this pretend pregnancy was so important to him. She should be the happiest woman alive, but unexpectedly Caroline felt like crying.

"I said a number of things," she told him, her gaze lowered to her clenched hands in her lap. "Not all of them were true." She dreaded telling him there wasn't any baby. False pretenses and disappointment—this was no way to negotiate a reconciliation. "How's Tanana?" she asked, changing the topic.

"Much better. She misses you and so do the others. Carl's growing every day."

"I...miss them too."

"Do...did you miss me?" he asked starkly.

He sounded so unsure of himself, so confused, that finding the words to tell him what was on her mind was impossible. Instead she nodded vigorously.

"I know I've made some mistakes.... I know I haven't got any business asking you to reconsider the divorce, but I love you, Caroline, and I'll do whatever you want to make things right between us."

"I know," she said miserably.

"If you know that, then why are you

acting like my being here is all wrong? It's that Larry guy, isn't it? You've started seeing him again, haven't you?"

"Yes…no. We went to one movie and I cried through the whole thing because I was so miserable without you. Finally Larry told me I should go back to you where I belong."

"He told you that?"

She nodded again.

"Is Alaska the problem, love? Would you rather we lived somewhere else?"

"No," she said quickly. "I love Alaska. It was the fever and the exhaustion and everything else that scared me off. You were right— a week after I got here, I knew Seattle would never be my home again. My home is with you."

"Oh, love, I've been going crazy without you. Nothing's good anymore unless you're there to share it with me." Although it was awkward in the front seat of the car, Paul gathered her in his arms and kissed her with the hunger of long absence. His mouth moved over hers slowly, sensuously, as though he couldn't believe she was in his arms and he was half afraid she'd disappear.

Caroline wrapped her arms around his neck and kissed him back with all the passion of the lonely weeks. Tears dampened her face and she buried her nose in his throat, heaving a sigh. "There's something you should know."

"What's that, love?"

"I...I didn't write the letter."

He went still. "What letter?"

"The one that told you I was pregnant."

Caroline could feel the air crack with electricity. The calm before the storm; the peace before the fury; the stillness before the outrage. She squeezed her eyes shut, waiting.

"You're not pregnant?"

"I swear I didn't know my aunts had

written to you. I can only apologize. If you want, I—"

"Love." His index finger under her chin raised her eyes to his. "I didn't receive any letter."

"You… What? No letter?"

"None."

"You mean… Oh, Paul, Paul." She spread kisses over his face. She kissed his eyes, his nose, his forehead, his chin and his mouth…. Again and again, until they were both winded and exhilarated.

"I didn't ever think I'd be thanking the postal service for their bi-weekly delivery," Paul said and chuckled.

"You love me more than Diane." She said it with wonder, as though even now she wasn't sure it could possibly be true.

"Of course. You're my wife."

"But…"

"Diane was a long time ago."

"But you saved things to remember her by."

"Only her letter. She decided she wasn't the type to live in the wilds of Alaska. She said if I loved her, I'd be willing to give up this craziness and come to her."

"But why keep the letter?"

"To remind me that it takes a special kind of person to appreciate the challenge of Alaska. It's not right for every woman, but it's right for you, Caroline."

"Because *you're* right for me." Her face shone with her love. She was so happy. So very happy...

"I can't promise you there won't be fevers or accidents or that things won't go wrong, but I vow I'll never leave you to face them alone and I'll never doubt you again."

"I promise you the same thing." She felt like singing and dancing and loving this man for the rest of her days. She placed her head on his shoulder and sighed. "Can we go home soon? I miss

Gold River. I want to spend Christmas there! With you."

"Yes, love. When would you like to go?"

"Is today too soon? Oh, Paul, I had the most marvelous idea about getting some additional medical training so we could open a permanent clinic."

He chuckled. "I sent for a mail-order bride, not a doctor."

"But I could've done so much more when the fever broke out if I'd had the proper supplies."

Paul's hand slipped under her sweater to caress her skin. "I have a feeling you're going to be too preoccupied for a while to be doing much studying."

"But it's a good idea, isn't it?"

"Yes, love. It is."

"Oh, Paul, thank you for loving me, thank you for coming for me and thank you for playing Scrabble with me."

"No, love," he said seriously. "Thank *you*."

With a happy, excited laugh, she hungrily brought her mouth to his.

"Merry Christmas, Caroline," he whispered a long moment later.

"Merry Christmas, Paul. This is the best Christmas gift I ever got."

"Me, too, love. Me, too."

* * * * *

The
ESSENTIAL COLLECTION

YES! Please send me the *Essential Collection by Debbie Macomber* in Larger Print. This collection begins with 3 FREE books and 2 FREE gifts in the first shipment, and more free gifts will follow! My books will arrive in 8 monthly shipments until I have the entire 51-book *Essential Collection by Debbie Macomber.* I will receive 2 or 3 FREE books in each shipment and I will pay just $4.99 U.S./$5.89 CDN. for each of the other 4 books in each shipment, plus $2.99 for shipping and handling. *If I decide to keep the entire collection, I'll have paid for only 32 books because 19 books are FREE! I understand that by accepting the 3 free books and gifts places me under no obligation to buy anything. I can always return a shipment and cancel at any time. My free books and gifts are mine to keep no matter what I decide.

261 HCN 1446   461 HCN 1446

Name _____ (PLEASE PRINT) _____

Address _____ Apt. # _____

City _____ State/Prov. _____ Zip/Postal Code _____

Signature (if under 18, a parent or guardian must sign) _____

Mail to the Harlequin® Reader Service:
IN U.S.A.: P.O. Box 1867, Buffalo, NY 14240-1867
IN CANADA: P.O. Box 609, Fort Erie, Ontario L2A 5X3

* Terms and prices subject to change without notice. Prices do not include applicable taxes. Sales tax applicable in N.Y. Canadian residents will be charged applicable taxes. This offer is limited to one order per household. All orders subject to approval. Credit or debit balances in a customer's account(s) may be offset by any other outstanding balance owed by or to the customer. Please allow 4 to 6 weeks for delivery. Offer available while quantities last. Offer not available to Quebec residents.

EDMBPA14